MICK BOGERMAN'S WARNING NOTE TO PARENTS:

Hey, parents! It's me, Mick Bogerman. I'm here to tell you this story is rated PG for werewolf-snarling peril and fork-stabbing dog fights. Beware, the clowns in this story will not make you giggle. They'd rather make you dinner. *Their* dinner, that is. The language is standard twelve-year-old name-calling, like dorkhead, boogerbreath, and slug-pie ugly, although I do make a special effort to stay clear of mom insults and potty jokes. As far as stupid romance, I tried my best to keep it out of this story, even though my friends had other ideas.

So if you're looking for a wimpy, child-type book, turn away now. But if your kid is not a wimp and likes a heart-pounding scare and chasing down hungry circus werewolves, then this, dear parent, is the story for your kid.

ALSO BY
MICK BOGERMAN

Slug Pie Story #1:

How to Navigate Zombie Cave and

Defeat Pirate Pete

Slug Pie Story #2:

How to Rid Your Swimming Pool of

a Bloodthirsty Mermaid

Slug Pie Story #3:

How to Destroy the New Girl's Killer

Robot Army

How to Protect Your Neighborhood from Circus Werewolves

Slug Pie Story #4

How to Protect Your Neighborhood from Circus Werewolves

Mick Bogerman

SLUG PIE STORIES, LLC/ FRANKFORT

Slug Pie Stories, LLC
8126 West Evergreen Drive
Frankfort, IL 60423

www.slugpiestories.com

Book design © 2013, BookDesignTemplates.com

Cover design and illustration © 2016, Kat Powell

Interior illustrations © 2016, Kat Powell

Frankfort / Mick Bogerman – First Edition

ISBN 978-0-9963325-2-1

Printed in the United States of America

For Cathy

STEP 1

Find a Ride

THE GUY WHO INVENTED spring break deserves a parade, or at least his face on one of those postage stamps Mrs. Shumaker collects. She could stick him between twenty-nine–cent Elvis and Superman 2006. Why not? He created the perfect mini-vacation, timed just right, between winter blahs and summer sweats.

If only it would get here already. I squirm at my desk, sniffing spring air through the cracked window, counting ceiling tiles, picking crud outta my nails with a paperclip, thinking I can't possibly take one . . . more . . . second . . . of Beachwood Middle School, and then the next thing I know—

"Well that's it," Mrs. Shumaker says. "Only half day today. We'll look at the Gettysburg Address when we get back. Have a nice break. I know I will."

I will too, Mrs. Shumaker. I will too.

This spring break is gonna be extra awesome. My two favorites are coming to town: Uncle George and the circus. Both are staying five whole days. Better still, this year's circus promises a bunch of new acts. They even changed their name from Auguste Linville Circus to A. Linville & Purnima Bros. Circus. I can't wait to find out what the Purnima brothers are all about.

After the school bus drops me at my stop, Neill Gillis calls through the bus window, "See you tonight, Mick!" I spin and give him a double thumbs-up before sprinting to my apartment building. All my friends are gonna be there for the circus's opening: Neill and Cooper, Booger-Face MacDougal, Brendan. Even PJ's coming 'cause his spring break from boarding school lines up with mine. And, of course, my little brother, Finley. He loves the circus as much as me.

Only my friend Savannah Diamond will be missing. Too bad Savannah and her parents already left for China. They're gonna be gone for the next couple weeks, adopting her a baby sister. Got no idea why they wanted a baby girl instead of a boy. Everyone knows boys are lots easier to take care of. We pretty much take care of ourselves, plus we're lots more fun to hang out with.

"You'll miss the tigers jumping through a hoop of flames," I told her before she left.

"I'm going to see the Great Wall and eat Mapo tofu."

Mapo tofu sounds about as tasty as tapioca pudding. That's been sitting out. For a month. "Well I'm gonna see the Great Hamdini, and me and Finley are gonna eat corn dogs and fried Twinkies until we barf."

"You're hopeless, Mick."

"Don't knock it till you've tried it."

She doesn't know what she's missing. Cotton candy puke comes out the same pink color as it does going in. This time me and Finley are gonna try blue.

My ring of keys jingles as I unlock the four padlocks on my front door. We've had extra security ever since an army of killer insect robots broke into our apartment last fall. Oh man, was that an adventure. They're long gone now thanks to me, Finley, and Savannah, so Mom really doesn't have to worry, but she wanted the locks anyway. She says they give her "peace of mind."

"OK," I keep telling her. "Suit yourself." I know better. Killer insect robots can laser off a "piece of your mind" whether you got four locks or four hundred.

As soon as I kick off my shoes to stretch my toes, the phone rings. I run to the kitchen, snatching the phone off the hook as I skid across the floor. The cord only stretches two feet before it threatens to tug the whole thing outta the wall. Sheesh, we're probably one of two families in all of North Carolina that still use a phone with wires.

"Hello?"

"Hey, Mick. You excited about this week?"

"Hey, Uncle George. You bet I am. When you getting here?"

"About that . . . Looks like I'm going to be delayed a few more days. I'll be there Tuesday."

"Oh."

He must recognize my disappointed voice 'cause he says, "I'm bummed too, buddy, but, hey, I'm bringing everything you put on your and Finley's wish list."

Yes! I don't know how he does it, but Uncle George always comes through. Me and Finley keep trying to stump him with hard-to-find items. But he *never* gets stumped. Got me the miner's hat and pitchfork I used in Zombie Cave last summer, and last fall he got me a brand new bike. I ended up giving the new bike to Finley, 'cause Savannah had already fixed my old broken one. No sense having two when there's only one of me. But now I have to carry a bike lock with me whenever I ride 'cause she turned my old bike into the best bike in town. Best in the whole county. She even gave it racing stripes. She's handy like that.

Uncle George is handy too. If he got me what I

hope he got me. My stomach's so squirmy I can hardly stand it. "A real bow? With real arrows?"

"Yep. I got something sweet for your mom, too. To make the arrows easier to live with."

"What? A Kevlar dress? Captain America's shield?"

"Suction-cup tips."

"Aw, man." I might as well trade my bike for a trike and drink out of a sippy cup.

"But just between you and me, I'll bring the real tips in a box. We'll do some target practice together."

"OK." That'll still be fun. Not as fun as slinging arrows through Beachwood like Hawkeye from the Avengers, protecting the innocent, and taking out the bad guys.

"So if you're not coming tonight, who's taking me and Finley to the circus?"

"You'll have to ride with one of your friends or wait until tomorrow when your mom's not working. Sorry, kiddo. See you when I get there."

His truck rumbles in the background before he clicks off.

Finley drops his backpack on the kitchen table and opens the fridge. "Who was that, Mopey Face?"

"I'm not mopey. And you need to stop using words like 'mopey.' Someone's gonna stuff you in your locker for it." He was pretty psyched when he moved up from a tote to a locker in fifth grade. I'd hate for his vocab to ruin it for him forever.

"You worry too much. I can take care of myself." He pours himself a glass of milk and starts slugging it down.

Don't I know it. My little brother's gotten me out of trouble more than once. "Uncle George can't come for another day. We gotta find a ride tonight."

Finley wipes his mouth with the back of his hand and refills his glass. "Ask PJ."

Yes! PJ is the richest kid in town. His parents got a garage as big as a house for all their fancy cars. PJ's got his own personal driver, for Pete's sake. He'll take us to the circus for sure.

"Here." I hand Finley the phone. "You call PJ. And then call Mom. Ask her if we can use the cookie jar money since Uncle George won't be here to pay for our tickets. I'm gonna get my stuff ready."

"Stuff? What do you have to bring to the circus 'sides yourself?"

"You'll see, little brother. You'll see."

STEP 2

Wear a Disguise

WHEN I STEP BACK into the kitchen, Finley takes one look at me and snorts milk out both his nostrils. "Ouch, that smarts." He rubs at his nose. "Why you dressed like that?"

"Like what?"

"Like mini–Mr. Corcoran."

Mr. Corcoran is one of my teachers. He's from England and has an English accent, which is pretty cool when you teach English. I stand straighter and adjust my tie. My feet shift inside the too-big dress shoes.

"I am finally gonna get inside the adults-only side-show tent."

Finley shakes his head. "Looking like *that*, the adults are gonna kick you out of the whole circus this time, not just their tent."

"Naw. This will work. Larry Zuchowski is my age,

and he said he dressed like this once and got in to see a rated-R movie."

"Mom says Larry started shaving when he was ten."

My brother's downer-fest doesn't discourage me one bit. "I borrowed this whole costume from the theater department. Look." A strip of fuzzy brown hair stretches across my palm. "Need your help putting this on so it's not crooked." I hold the strip under my nose to show him where it's gonna go.

Finley snorts again. This time the milk makes it across the kitchen table. "You're killing me. A moustache? No one's gonna believe that's really yours."

"Sure they will. It'll be dark. These shoes got lifts in them. I showed the costume to Booger-Face, and he said I look like Robert Downy Jr. when he isn't pretending to be Iron Man."

"If Robert Downy Jr. was twelve and sneezed up a caterpillar." Finley snatches a paper towel from the roll and starts wiping up snotty milk.

"Come on. Help. It'll be so worth it. The Three-Eyed Lady. Dog Boy. Shrunken-Head Man. Live and up close. I'll tell you all about it. Or maybe once I'm in, I can sneak you in too. Come on."

"All right. I'll help you get your moustache on. But soon as we get there, I'm not hanging with you. You don't know me."

Yeah, well I remember thinking the same thing about Finley when he was six and still carried his blankie everywhere, but I don't say anything. He'll be jealous when I get to shake hands with Mighty Max, the world's strongest ninety-year-old man. The guy can pull a truck with his teeth.

The moustache feels like a line of ants marching underneath my nose. Takes all my effort not to scratch the thing off.

❖ ❖ ❖

"Hey, Mick, I didn't know we were dressing up. Who're you supposed to be?" PJ says as we climb into the back of his chauffeured sedan. "You kinda look like my parents' accountant, only younger. Much younger."

PJ's pasty-white skin glows by car light. He needs to get outside more; he could pass as a vampire. Not the sparkly kind the girls are always talking about on the bus ride home. The I'm-so-pale-'cause-I-sleep-inside-a-coffin-during-the-day kind.

I keep my thoughts to myself. Me and him have been making efforts to get along. Mom says we're like oil and water. In mom-talk I think that means we don't mix, or we're opposites, or something like that. Savannah said we should be commended for being open to socioeconomic diversity. "PJ's not diverse," I told her. "He's just not the same as me." Then she punched me in the arm for some strange reason.

"Mick's trying to look like an adult," Finley volunteers as he slides across the smooth leather seat.

PJ scrunches his nose. "Hmm." He tilts his head and squints at me. "Maybe. It *is* getting dark."

"You two are no help at all."

Gene, the driver, looks at us reflected in his rearview mirror. "What exactly are you trying to accomplish, Mr. Mick?"

"He wants to get into the adults-only sideshow tent," Finley announces. "He wants to look eighteen."

"I see. Well, good luck to you." Gene puts the car into gear and pulls away from the curb, a smile curling the corners of his mouth. It's one of the things I like about Gene. He doesn't shoot me down, or laugh, or make me go back to the apartment to change clothes. Not a lot of adults are like that.

It doesn't take us long to get to the circus, but since the police won't let Gene drop us off at the gate, we gotta park in the field with everyone else. Takes us nearly a whole ten minutes to walk to the front of the county fairgrounds 'cause it's so crowded. Looks like the whole town turned out for opening night.

The temperature drops as the sun creeps down.

I loosen my tie to let some of the cool air slip inside my stuffy shirt. How can adults dress like this and not melt into a puddle?

As we get closer, the music's louder and the people's voices sound like gulls fighting over crackers on the beach. Circus tents covered in lights stretch into the sky. This is so much better than taking the bus out to the convention center. Out here in the open air, excitement scurries under my skin like an electric current.

"You got your cell phone, PJ?" Gene asks as he pulls out his own phone.

"Yes."

"All right, then. I'll check-text you at 7:00 p.m. on the dot, and then again at 8:30. Last performances end at 9:45, so we'll meet up here at the front gate, say 10:00? Give you a chance to get through the crowds. Four hours should be plenty of time to catch a couple of the shows and eat yourselves sick."

"What're you going to do, Gene?" PJ tucks his phone into a pack he's wearing strapped to his waist. A *fanny* pack. Jeez, I gotta have a talk with this kid.

"Me?" Gene says. "Thought I might check out that adults-only sideshow tent myself. See what all the fuss is about. Maybe I'll see you there, Mick." He winks and strides off, his dark form disappearing into the crowd.

Finley inhales, and his face breaks into a ginormous grin. "Smell that?"

I take a whiff too. At first my nose catches what must be the tiger cage. Then the breeze shifts and there's no mistaking the smell of fried heaven dusted with cinnamon sugar.

"Elephant ears!" me and Finley say together. Not to be confused with funnel cakes, which are a totally different thing. Elephant ears look like, well, elephant ears.

"I'm gonna get mine with strawberries and whipped cream. Come on, PJ." The three of us tear off toward the food vendors.

While we're standing in the longest line ever, I overhear some lady trying to comfort her kid. I can't help listening. For one, they're awful loud, and for two, PJ and Finley are talking about his boarding school, which is about the most boring conversation in the history of boredom and conversations.

The lady keeps saying, "Hush now, honey," in between the little kid's sobs. Then she says, "It's just face paint. They don't mean to be scary. Clowns are supposed to cheer you up."

"But, Mama, the tall one had teeth. Big teeth." The kid starts sobbing again.

A clown with teeth?

Cool.

Sounds like visiting the clown tent is next on my list.

"Hey, Mick! What's up with the 'stache?" Neill slides to one side of me, and Booger-Face takes the other side.

"Looks like you took a face dive in a barrel of wooly bears and one got stuck. Here, let me get it for you."

I bat Booger-Face's hand away before he rips off my disguise.

"I get it. You're pretending to be that old-time comic guy. Groucho, right?" Neill takes a bite out of a corn dog dripping mustard down his wrist.

"You won't be laughing when I get into the side-show tent this year."

"Booger-Face already tried. He didn't get two steps next to the entrance 'fore two big guys grabbed him and–"

"Yeah, yeah. I got closer than last year." Booger-Face shrugs. "Anyhoo, the sideshow tent's old news. This year it's the clown show we've got to see. The Purnima brothers are all everyone's talking about. Kids come out of their show either crying or screaming. Bunch of folks left. Lots of parents are keeping their kids away. We gotta see it before my mom says I can't."

I scan the area where the kid and her mom were a minute ago, but they're gone now. Wonder if they went home already. The lines do seem to be getting shorter. The crowd's thinning out. That *is* strange since it's still early.

"Cooper texted. He's gonna meet us at the clown show. Marissa's hanging with her cousin. Hey, did you know she asked Neill to that spring dance coming up? The one where the girls ask the guys. Neill's such a hot catch he got asked early." Booger-Face slaps Neill on the back.

"Cut it out. I haven't said yes. She should've asked Cooper. He's the one has a crush on her. Are you going, Mick?" Neill looks at me like I got all the answers.

"No. Dances are stupid." There. Now we can have a good time talking about anything else.

Of course Finley's gotta put his two cents in. "Mick's scared of dancing. He hopes nobody asks him."

"Don't worry, Mick. Girls don't like you." Booger-Face's thumbs peck at his phone. "Savannah's outta town so she's not coming. Brendan couldn't come tonight either. He's got a piano recital. Whose place we gonna sleep at tonight? My mom wants to know."

"I have plenty of room at my house. Gene can drive us."

"PJ's place it is."

"I already told Brendan that Cooper and me would stay with him tonight." Neill licks at the mustard on his sleeve. "Maybe next time."

"We'll still have fun with four. Right, Mick?" Booger-Face stuffs his phone in his back pocket. No fanny pack for him.

"You bet." I let Booger-Face's comment about girls not liking me slide right off my back. I got better things to do than think about girls. Like hanging at PJ's house. There's no way *not* to have fun at PJ's. He's got a Recreation and Entertainment Center filled with video games, a pool table, a bunch of pinball machines, and a giant-screen TV. He's got a walk-in pantry as big as my kitchen and a nanny who'll cook up anything we want. Shoot, we skateboarded in his entrance hall over Christmas break. As long as we stay away from the swimming pool. We've been grounded from PJ's pool ever since we tossed a bloodthirsty mermaid into the deep end and she stained it black with her squid ink.

At last I make it to the front of the food line. Since the cookie jar money paid for entrance tickets, I have to use my own money to eat. The birthday cash I've been saving slides easy on the counter, and two elephant ears doused in strawberries and covered with towering mounds of whipped cream land in my outstretched hands. Cinnamon steam bathes my face as I hand Finley his.

We wait for PJ while he gets an electric-blue slushy and then complains about the brain freeze. His pinkie shoots out when he grips his straw. He notices me noticing and tucks the flyaway finger back in. With breeding and boarding school working against us, it's gonna take me and Finley years to help PJ break his rich-kid habits.

Booger-Face swallows half a fried Twinkie in a single bite. Sponge and cream squeeze out the corners of his mouth. PJ grins at him and shows off his Smurf-stained teeth. Maybe Booger-Face'll be the one to rub off on PJ.

Now that all five of us have something tasty stuffed into our faces, we head off to the clown tent, tinny circus music leading the way. Scattered popcorn and peanut shells imbedded in the dirt crunch under our shoes.

I scan the crowd for Cooper. No sign of him yet, but he might already be inside. More lights flicker on as night settles in. Clouds coat the moon. A cool breeze swipes my sweat away and makes the tent fabric rustle.

"This is great," Finley whispers by my side as we shuffle inside with a small crowd. A whipped cream grin stretches across his face.

"You bet." I grin back at him. "Let's see those clowns."

STEP 3

Watch the Clown Show

FOR A TWELVE-YEAR-OLD, a clown show is kinda lame. Finley still likes them, but he's only ten. He still thinks WWE wrestling is real. If it weren't for the wild rumors about this particular clown show, I'd have steered clear.

The clowns are not lame tonight.

Tonight, I have to admit, they grab my attention right from the start and hold on barnacle-tight.

After Auguste Linville announces the Purnima brothers with his huge megaphone, the dorky circus music starts. Seven clowns tumble into the ring. They've got the standard white-painted faces, purple-and-green fluffy hair, and red-bulb noses, but, well, these guys aren't exactly clown sized. They're built like the linebackers from the Carolina Panthers.

"Wow. Supersize." Booger-Face stuffs a handful of

popcorn into his mouth, but he's not talking about food portions. "Wouldn't want to call them clowns to their faces."

"They don't act like clowns," Finley whispers to me. "Aren't they supposed to ride tiny trikes and throw buckets of sparkles at each other?"

Can't decide what to tell him. *Duck* comes to mind, 'cause they're throwing things at each other, all right: metal spears, giant knives, Ninja stars, an axe. They're not good at it, either.

The clown with the purple polka-dotted suit lobs a knife looks like an Arabian sword. The blade does sparkle as it spins, but then it slices through another clown's suspenders, nearly filleting him. The largest clown of them all gets a reverse mohawk when a spear shaves through his wig. Another clown looks like he loses a piece of earlobe after a dagger nicks him. The blood trickle shows up good against his white-painted face.

"Did you see that?" I ask Finley.

"Uh-huh. 'Cept he's healed. Look."

When I look again, the guy's fine. Earlobe back on his ear. Blood nowhere to be seen. "It's a trick. Gotta be."

Audience participation time is especially scary. We're all volunteers, no matter how much we try to shrink and disappear behind the family in front of us.

Booger-Face nearly shakes out of his skin when a Ninja star clips off that pesky chunk of hair he's always swiping at. Star and hair embed in the empty riser behind us.

"I don't feel so good." He hands off his popcorn to PJ. "How much longer?"

"It's only been ten minutes."

Next they drag out and assemble a couple really tall ladders. Then they position some really small containers. I swear it's impossible to walk away after swan-diving from twenty stories into a kid's plastic pool, but one clown does it. All the while, his tongue is hanging through a foam-coated, painted grin, like a circus dog with rabies.

"Did you hear his bones crack?" Finley whispers next to me. "I think he broke some of his bones."

"Sound effects," I tell him, 'cause that's what I want to believe.

I cringe as another clown threads a thin rope through his nose and then pulls the end outta the opposite nostril like he's flossing his sinuses.

"Ugh! I think I'm gonna barf," Neill says while we watch a clown swallow a light bulb and then cough it back up. Not a little night-light bulb, either. A full-sized, 60-watt, light-up-the-family-room kind of bulb.

"This isn't like any clown show I've ever seen."

PJ's eyes are wide and staring as he slurps on the last centimeter of his slushy.

Me either.

"Do you think that's a real staple gun that guy's using on his head? With real staples?" Cooper asks. "Marissa said that Chase told her that his older brother's friend Mark almost lost the tip of his finger to a staple gun. Getting stapled must really hurt. The red stuff trickling down that clown's head . . . blood or syrup?"

"Barbecue sauce. Has to be. This is all done with makeup and optical illusion. No one's gonna staple his head for real. That'd be—"

"Crazy," Booger-Face interrupts me. "These clowns are crazy."

The family of four sitting to my left makes their exit. The kids hide their eyes behind their hands as their parents lead them away. Cooper looks like he wants to follow 'em out. But I have to stay. I got a reputation to maintain.

Two of the clowns drive a small truck with a cannon on the back into the tent. Must be time for the grand finale. I've seen this before. They use compressed air to propel a human cannonball about a hundred feet into a net. Firecrackers make the sound and smoke. They're supposed to make you think real fire and gunpowder are being used. Circus people have been doing this act forever.

This cannon's not painted with stars and polka dots though. Cast-iron black, the thing looks like it rolled off a pirate ship. Only it's bigger—much bigger. A clown wearing purple suspenders climbs into the opening, while another holds a torch. Looks like they're gonna light this fuse for real instead of using a detonator.

"Where's the net?" Finley asks.

Before I can answer, the explosion rattles the bleachers and makes the tent fabric sway.

A clown-shaped meteor rockets across the tent and slams into a . . . a wall. Not a net, not even a trampoline tipped on its side. A thick, wooden wall. Then he tucks and rolls to the ground.

He's on fire.

"They gonna put him out?" Finley grabs my shirt sleeve.

"Yeah, yeah. Of course."

But no one comes running with a fire extinguisher. No one brings a bucket of water. My guts do a couple backflips.

A woman screams. Kids start crying. A man—jeez, it's my school's principal, Mr. Nuñez—stands and starts moving like he's gonna do something if no one else will.

Both Neill and Cooper look at me with panic planted on their faces. I can't see PJ's face 'cause he's hiding it behind his hands just like those little kids. Booger-Face is talking quiet to him, trying to calm him.

The clown is still on fire.

"Let's get outta here," I say. This is too much for Finley.

The six of us start weaving our way down the risers, when suddenly the clown gets up and starts dancing like he's wearing an old disco suit instead of flames.

"What?" Booger-Face holds out his arms to stop us.

Burning Clown Guy sheds his fiery clothes and stands in the center ring in nothing but a pair of white boxers covered in red hearts.

I think he says, "Ta-da!" Beside him, his clothes smolder in a lump.

Some people laugh nervously. A few people clap. Most are like me—high-tailing it out of there.

❖ ❖ ❖

"What was that? What was that? What? What? What?" Cooper stomps around in the gravel. "I smelled burnt hair. Did you smell burnt hair? How could he be burning up one minute and then OK the next? I know what I saw. I know what I heard. Blood and busted bones.

That guy who jumped into the wading pool? He landed on his head. Marissa told me that Mr. Corcoran told her that head injuries are serious business. That clown should be in a hospital. How is that possible he's not in an ambulance going to the hospital? How is *he* possible?"

Neill paces next me. "Had to be illusions. Like Mick said. Like what Criss Angel and David Blaine do."

"That *definitely* wasn't like any clown show I've ever seen." PJ crosses his arms in front of his chest. "They weren't very funny."

I break in to the conversation. "I heard a kid crying about this show to his mom. He said the clowns had teeth. Wonder what he meant by that. I saw a lot of weird, but no teeth."

Booger-Face nods. "Yeah, I heard something like that. My seven-year-old neighbor went to the first show. When she and her dad were leaving, one of the clowns got real close to her face and then he growled at her. She saw blood on his face, and his breath made her gag. She didn't mention the teeth. But I'm with you and Neill. It's all fake."

"It's not fake. It's Wolverine."

"What'd you say?"

We all turn to Finley.

"The clowns. They're like Wolverine. They really do

get hurt, but they heal fast. Like a . . . mutant."

The clown who lost his earlobe. And the clown with broken bones. One minute they're busted up, and the next they look like nothing happened. It *is* kinda like Wolverine. But the guys sure don't seem interested in hearing about it.

"Good one, Finley," Booger-Face slaps him on the back. "Where should we go next? Aerial acrobats? The Great Hamdini? Mighty Max? They pulled him out of the adults-only tent this year, so we can see him now. How 'bout the tiger show?"

"They don't have a tiger show this year. You can only watch 'em get fed. My mom says that her friend told her that next year they're not bringing the tigers at all." Cooper goes on, 'cause that's what he does. "My mom said that her friend told her a lot of circuses are getting rid of all their wild animal acts."

I guess they figure they don't need wild animals when they got the Purnima brothers.

Neill pulls out a circus program. "There's Marco and Tamela Brisbane in tent C in fifteen minutes. 'Featuring juggling and equilibristics.' That means juggling with gymnastics. Let's go there."

"Finley, what do you want to do?" I ask. I decide that putting that clown show behind us is probably a good idea. I'll have to remember to ask Finley about his

Wolverine comment later when we're alone.

"The jugglers would be OK I guess."

"Great. The guys'll look after you. I have something I need to do." I whisper in Finley's ear, "Stay away from the clown tent, OK?"

He nods. "Where you goin'?"

I stand up straight and adjust my tie. "Time for me to walk right into the adults-only sideshow tent."

STEP 4

Persuade the Guard

AN ALMOST-FULL MOON brightens my path like a spotlight leading the way. A hand-painted sign squeaks as it swings between two thick metal poles outside the adults-only tent. The tent isn't actually called "the adults-only tent." The sign says it's Madam Mayhem's Macabre Pavilion. MUST BE 18 OR OLDER is scrawled underneath in drippy red paint.

There's no line. In fact, this side of the fairgrounds is nearly empty, 'cept for me and the guy busting out of a too-small tuxedo, leaning on a podium outside the entrance flap. A crooked top hat perches on his shaggy gray hair.

When I walk by all casual-like, the dress shoes I'm wearing slip and slide on the gravel. My duck waddle definitely interferes with my disguise. Some-how, I keep my balance and peek into the entrance with my peripheral vision. Dark and super-still, not even a shadow's moving inside the tent.

On my second pass by, I get a look inside the tent from a different angle. Maybe I'll glimpse the Real Pan, a guy with goat horns and hooves, or the two-headed pelican. Nope. More dark. Even when I tilt my head.

"Hey, kid! You gonna try to get in, or you just gonna pace in front of me?" Top Hat Guy's voice booms.

I point to myself and mouth, "Who? Me?"

"Yeah. You. The kid in the suit. The one with the fake moustache."

Pushing back my shoulders and puffing out my chest, I sidle over to the podium. If I'm gonna do this right, I gotta own my disguise. "This is not a fake moustache, and I am not a kid," I say in my best baritone voice.

He frowns and his forehead looks like an accordion. "Right. You know, I can get you thrown in jail for impersonating an adult. One button pressed on my cell and the cops'll be all over you."

"Yeah, I'm gonna go now."

"Hey, kid." He smiles, revealing broken yellow teeth. "You got guts getting all decked out in a suit and tie. Palm me a twenty and I'll let you in after the last event when folks are clearing out."

Jeez, does this guy need to cut back on the jawbreakers. "All I got is a ten." I finger my last bill inside my pocket.

He scans me and shakes his head. The top hat shifts to the left, but amazingly, it doesn't fall. "Not worth it. Twenty or nothing."

Uncle George once told me that when you're negotiating a better deal, you gotta be ready to walk away. If the other guy gets even a whiff you're gonna waffle, a twenty will turn into two twenties.

I start shuffling off. "I told you all I got is a ten," I say over my shoulder.

A torn tent seam catches my attention. The frayed ends are dancing in a spring breeze. There's my plan B. I'll come back later and slip right in.

I'm almost round the long end of the tent when the guy hollers after me, "Come back at 9:30. I'll let you in for ten bucks."

Ha! Uncle George was right again.

❖ ❖ ❖

I gotta wait outside Marco and Tamela Brisbane's tent for Finley and the rest of the guys to finish watching the show. My moustache peels off without taking any skin. I tuck it next to the ten-dollar bill. The money's practically smoking 'cause it wants to escape my pocket so bad. The vendor next to me is stirring up a batch of kettle corn, and the sweet-n-salty smell fills my mouth with saliva. I'd rather fill my mouth with kettle corn, but I'm so close to getting into that adults-only tent. I swallow hard.

Finley gives me a jab in the arm and breaks my sugarcoated trance. "Did they think you were eighteen? Did they let you in? "

I glance at PJ and Cooper. They don't look upset or sick to their stomachs, so equilibristics with the Brisbanes must've gone OK. Other people are leaving the tent with smiles on their faces instead of scowls and tears. Looks like the Purnima clowns are the only act terrifying the people of Beachwood tonight.

"Well?" Booger-Face asks.

The guys have me surrounded.

"The guard's gonna let me in after the last show lets out. If I give him all of my money."

"Wow. You bribed him?" Neill says.

"He suggested it." More like demanded it.

"Extortion, then."

"Yeah, I guess so. Anyway, once I'm in, I'm gonna let you guys in too. There's a torn seam on the left side of the tent, near the back, a couple feet off the ground. I'll wave you through when it's clear. We'll all get to see what's inside Madam Mayhem's Macabre Pavilion."

Finley and the guys grin at me like I told them they'd won the lottery. I'm definitely earning rep points tonight.

"What'll we do until then?" PJ looks at his watch. "We have time for one more show."

Neill smoothes his crumpled circus map. "Mad Max's tent is next to Madam Mayhem's. Let's see him and bug out a few minutes early so we're in position when Mick gives us the signal."

"What's the signal gonna be, Mick? Remember when Mrs. Shumaker said the Native Americans used signals and sign language? She showed us this one in class." Cooper puts both fists near his chest and then thrusts them forward a few inches. "It means 'go ahead.' Can you do that through the gap in the tent? Then we'll know it's safe."

"Uh, sure." I'd have to grow an extra set of arms to hold open the flap for them to see *that* signal, but hey, whatever floats Cooper's boat.

❖ ❖ ❖

Ten dollars later, Top Hat Guy sneaks me in to Madam Mayhem's tent. I only have a half hour before Gene'll be looking for us. It works out to be even less time than that 'cause the performers are already packing up for the night. Plus I promised to let Finley and the guys in through the rip in the tent. We'll be lucky to see anything.

On my way to the torn part of the tent, I pass the Three-Eyed Lady. She's easy to spot in a red sparkly gown, sitting on a wooden stool, pulling off her pointy heels. Her black hair is pulled away from her face with a headband so I can easily see her third eye set into the center of her forehead. Even though two of her eyes look at her bare feet while she rubs them, that third eyeball tracks me.

"Who let you in here, baby? Come on over and let me get a look at you." She starts laughing like she's the world's funniest comedienne.

My head says to get while the gettin's good, but my feet have other ideas. They walk me right up to the lady with three eyes, all of them looking at me now. Can't tell what color they are 'cause the light's dim. They look kinda gray, and kinda tired, each one framed with makeup.

"What's your name, baby?"

Maybe I'll give her a fake name. "Mick," rolls outta my mouth. Yes. I am a truth-spewing dorkhead who can't invent a fake name on the spot.

"I'm Carlotta." She extends her hand, a hundred bracelets clanking on her wrist.

My hand seems to be the only thing I have control over tonight. It's glued to my side. Talking to the Three-Eyed Lady is one thing. Letting her grab my hand and pull me in close? No thanks.

Her three eyes narrow. She rests her hand in the lap of her dress. "Well, Mick, you better move along before Rocky sees you. He likes to toss babies."

"Rocky?"

"There he is. Shoo!"

I trot to the long edge of the tent and peek over my shoulder. Shrunken-Head Man joins Carlotta and kneels to help her put her shoes back on. He's been mislabeled for sure. His head looks normal-sized to me. It's his body that's H-U-G-E. A toss from him and I'd probably beat Savannah to the Great Wall of China. She'd show up with her parents for a tour, and I'd have to explain how I got there. No thanks. I back up, then turn and sneak off.

The tiny lights strung throughout the place are more for decoration than actual lighting. Takes me a few minutes to find the torn seam. There it is! Near a metal cage that smells like my neighbor's dog, Bagel Boy, when he hasn't had a bath for a while. Yeah, that dog has the stupidest dog name in the history of stupid dog names. I would've named him Buddy or Jake. Those are good dog names. Not Bagel Boy.

I can't see what's in the cage, but I give it a wide berth anyway. I thrust my head and shoulders through the tear in the tent fabric and try to give the Native American signal for "go ahead."

Cooper shakes his head. "You're doing it wrong. Mrs. Shumaker said the Native Americans hold their thumbs on the outside of their fists. Like this."

Oly moly, Cooper Schwartz, I'm about to give you the hand signal for a punch in the nose. I duck back inside and hold open the fabric so everyone can climb into the tent.

"What took you so long?" Booger-Face says loud enough for anyone to hear.

"Shh. We're not supposed to be here. Remember?"

He slips through the gap and helps me hold it for Cooper, Neill, and Finley. PJ struggles and tumbles onto his knees and elbows with an *ooph*!

"You OK?" Finley asks.

"Yes." He brushes himself off and then crinkles his nose. "What is that smell?"

"It's coming from the cage over there." I point to the darkened shape.

Booger-Face pulls a set of keys from his pocket.

"You going in?"

"Naw, you goober. *Lookin'* in." He clicks on a small flashlight hooked to the key ring and points the light at the cage.

At first all I notice is a flash of brightness.

Finley gasps, and that's when I realize what I'm looking at.

There's a redheaded boy huddled on the ground. His back's to us, and he's wearing torn shorts and a dirty, torn shirt. His skin is scuffed and smudged like he's been in a fight. A coiled garden hose sits outside the bars, and the inside of the cage is a muddy mess. There's a gnawed bone and a metal water dish in the corner.

Booger-Face shines the light on a painted sign strung above the cage's padlocked entrance.

DOG BOY.

"Dog Boy?" Neill says. "He doesn't look like a dog."

The boy turns to face us, his skin blazing white in Booger-Face's light. He shields his eyes with his arm.

"Don't shine it right at him!" PJ tries to swipe at the flashlight. Booger-Face points the light at the ground instead.

"How come he's in a cage?" Finley asks me.

The boy in the cage stares at me like I know the answer.

"I don't know."

A trick of the light makes the boy's eyes glow a weird-looking green.

My feet propel me closer.

The boy pivots and rises so his whole body turns toward us. He's shorter than Finley. Can't be more than eight, maybe nine years old. I see the shackle on his ankle before I hear the clink of his chain.

Finley grabs my shirt sleeve again. He's starting to stretch it out. "He's a prisoner."

The boy in the cage sniffles and extends his hands, palms up. "Help me," he whispers in a hoarse voice. "I want to go home."

Rescue Dog Boy

THE CAGE DOOR RATTLES when I shake it, but it doesn't budge. Without a hacksaw, or a key, there's no way Dog Boy's getting out.

Neill elbows me. "We don't know anything about this kid. He might be locked up for a good reason. What're you gonna do with him if you get him out? You don't even know where his home *is* to get him to it."

"Don't talk about him like he's not there." PJ stands on the other side of me. "He can hear everything you say. Hey, are you hungry?" PJ unzips his fanny pack and pulls out ... a King-Size Almond Joy.

"Are you kidding me? Almond Joy?" Leave it to PJ to carry around the worst candy ever created. Obviously those candy makers didn't have kids on their minds when they stuffed coconut into perfectly good chocolate. "Don't you like Snickers?" Now there's a real candy bar.

"Hershey's bars!" Cooper chimes in. "What if Dog Boy has a peanut allergy? Like Marissa. Samantha says Marissa can't hardly eat any chocolate candy 'cause she's allergic to peanuts. Samantha says Marissa can't even be at our same lunch table if we're gonna eat Snickers."

"Skittles? Twizzlers? Fun Dip?" So many non-nut, non-gross choices.

"But I like the coconut."

Of course PJ would like coconut. My shoulders shudder. I bet the Mapo tofu Samantha's eating in China's got coconut in it too.

Neill turns the candy over in PJ's hands and reads the nutrition label with the flashlight. "Coconut doesn't count as a nut. I think it's a fruit. Should be OK."

"It's a drupe. Three things: a fruit, a nut, and a seed." PJ examines our reactions and his eyebrows stitch together. "What? You've never heard of a drupe? Don't you go to school?"

"Not *boarding* school." No, I attend the public school where they dropped drupe lessons in favor of Native American sign language.

A whisper escapes from the cage. "I'll take it."

"What?"

"The candy," Dog Boy says. "I'll take it."

PJ sticks his hand through the bars. The boy tries to grasp the wrapper, but his chain keeps him from reaching it.

"Toss it, PJ."

The candy lands at the boy's feet. "Oh, wait. Use this first." A small plastic bottle smacks the ground next to the candy.

"Hand sanitizer?" What else does PJ have stashed in his fanny pack? Rubber gloves? Pine-Sol?

"Well look how dirty he is. I wouldn't want him to get sick."

I shake my head at PJ. A moment later, the sounds of ripping and snarling yank my eyeballs back to the boy. He's tearing into the candy like a starving lion. Wrapper and chocolate stick to his teeth. Then he starts gnawing on the bottle of hand sanitizer, puncturing the plastic with his super-pointy canines. Gel squirts from his mouth and runs down his chin. Now I know how he got his name. He eats like a Rottweiler.

"Are you seeing this, Finley?"

That's when I realize we're short two people. Finley and Booger-Face are missing—have been missing for I don't know how long.

Panic hugs me like a grizzly bear. Just when I'm about to scream Finley's name and alert all circus personnel that a bunch of kids snuck inside their tent, I see him. He's running toward me, Booger-Face struggling to keep up, and in Finley's hand: a giant, jangling ring of keys.

"Where've you been? You can't disappear without telling me. Where'd you get those?"

"No time. Help me find the right one." He hands off the ring. I start shuffling through thirty keys, searching for one marked with a dog, or a bone, or a letter D—something, anything, 'cause every key looks exactly the same.

Booger-Face catches his breath. "You gotta try 'em all till you find it." He snatches the ring from my hand.

"Hey!"

He jams a key into the lock. Nothing. He tries the next one. Then the next. And the next. Triple nothing. This is gonna take all night, and from the sound of approaching footsteps, we don't got all night.

"Hurry."

"Give me a break." Booger-Face tugs another key.

Neill fumbles for the keys. "Let me try."

Booger-Face shoulders him off. "I got this."

Yeah. But he doesn't, 'cause he drops the all-look-alike, never-gonna-find-the-right-one keys on the ground.

"Ah, farts. I gotta start over." Booger-Face shakes the dirt from the keys.

"They're coming." Now Finley's hand is a vise through my shirt, clamping down on my arm.

Cooper's feet start dancing in place. "Who's coming?"

"Keep trying," I tell Booger-Face.

"It's this one. I know it."

It's not.

"This one."

No again.

"Come on." Neill kicks the cage. "Leave him. We gotta go. If we get caught—"

"We can't leave him." PJ stomps.

"We still gotta get his chain off." Finley's holding me so tight he's cutting off the blood circulating to my hand.

My fingers go numb. Then I hear voices. Getting louder. I recognize the sound of Shrunken-Head Man talking to another guy.

"Give the keys to me," Dog Boy growls.

Like a snake, my arm shakes off Finley and darts between Neill and Booger-Face. Pins and needles stab my hand as it wakes up from Finley's clutches, but I manage to snag the keys from Booger-Face and toss them to the boy.

He splays them on the ground and snatches the third from the left. In the time it takes my heart to *thumpa thump*, the shackles are in a lump at his feet.

Takes him two more heartbeats to lean against the cage and reach through the bars.

The six of us back away as he bends his wrist like a contortionist, jams a key into the padlock, twists, and—

"You kids! Get away from him!"

"Run!" PJ shrieks.

Cooper and Neill are already halfway to our exit when the lock pops and the cage door bangs open.

"Come on." Dog Boy holds open the torn tent seam. "If they catch you, they'll eat you."

"You're fast." Finley gives Dog Boy the once-over, and then he crawls through the opening after Neill. Cooper's feet shuffle outside, waiting.

"How'd you move like that? I didn't even see you get past me." Booger-Face shakes his head at Dog Boy and then follows Finley.

"Don't let them get away!" Shrunken-Head Man is one leap away. Strong hands grab my shoe.

Dog Boy grasps my shirt collar, lifting me off the ground. He push-pulls us both through the tent opening.

"My shoe!" It's gone.

"Leave it."

A thousand questions race through my head, but I can't ask any of them 'cause the guys chasing us, well they're still chasing us. Shrunken-Head Man's head pops outta the tent, but his shoulders are so large he can't advance. The tent shakes with his struggling.

We don't wait to see if he pulls the tent down around himself. I wish I hadn't eaten the whole elephant ear, 'cause my stomach's churning in time with my heartbeat. Running with one shoe off and one shoe on slows me down, but I don't want to take even ten seconds to kick off the other shoe.

"Hurry up, Cinderella!" Booger-Face tosses over his shoulder.

"I'm right behind you!"

By the time we get to the front gate, I can barely squeeze in a breath. Finley's face shines with sweat. PJ sounds like he's gonna cough out a lung.

Dog Boy's nostrils flare. "They're coming."

I scan the thinning crowd. Families reuniting. Friends saying good-bye. No Shrunken-Head Man. No circus thugs. "Where?"

Dog Boy inhales noisily. He tilts his head, his eyes bright. "They've told Mr. Linville. He's sending the brothers. We have about a minute before they come around that tent." He points directly in front of us.

"How does he know that?" Cooper hugs himself. He's shivering so hard his teeth click like someone's typing on a keyboard inside his head. "How do you know that?"

"I hear them. And I smell them."

"Oh." Cooper's voice comes out soft and tiny and trembling.

I peel off the coat that got me into the adults-only tent in the first place and drape it around Cooper's shoulders. "You can give it back after break."

"Oh." His shaking drops a notch. "Thanks."

"Um, yeah. I see my parents. Come on, Cooper." Neill waves to his dad, who's easy to spot 'cause he stands a head taller than everyone around him. "Call me later, Mick. I'll be at Brendan's. Let me know what happens with . . . your new friend."

Neill dashes off, pulling Cooper along with him. The last I see, they're both tugging Neill's parents into the parking lot, throwing frightened glances over their shoulders.

PJ tucks his phone back into his fanny pack. "Gene's pulling the car around."

"Go. Now!" Dog Boy pushes each of us in turn, fast and strong, like he's rounding up sheep. We sprint out the gate, elbowing people, threading between parked cars. My gaze catches PJ's black sedan inching forward.

"Over here." The car rolls to a stop next to me, and I yank the back door open. "Get in. Get in!"

The five of us pour inside.

Just before PJ slams the door shut, a howl pierces the night, sending shivers from the top of my head down to the tip of my shoeless foot.

"They're angry." Dog Boy's eyes flash that creepy green color. "Drive fast or they'll catch me again."

"What on earth? You boys in trouble?"

Another howl, muffled by the closed door, but closer this time.

"Go, Gene. GO!"

Gene doesn't say more. He slams the car into gear. The wheels spin and we tear out of the grassy parking lot, throwing sod clods behind us. My heart thunders inside my ribcage. We swerve to avoid pedestrians, cars, the police directing traffic, until we finally hit pavement and then the open road.

Finley exhales next to me. Booger-Face slumps in the seat. PJ unclenches his hands, and Dog Boy stares out the window. Not me. I can't relax. Not now. Maybe not ever. There's one thought gripping my brain tighter than Finley on my arm. Something Dog Boy said while we made our escape.

If they catch you, they'll eat you.

STEP 6

Cover the Scent

"OPEN THE WINDOW!" Dog Boy suddenly shouts.

"You carsick?" After scarfing down a candy bar in its wrapper and a hand sanitizer dessert, I can't blame the kid if he's queasy. Running from howling clowns's got my stomach knotted up like fishing net.

Gene presses a button, and crisp night air rushes inside.

"Stick your head out," PJ says. "My father will flip if you vomit on the leather upholstery."

"Ugh. If you puke, I'll puke. Mister, you better open my window too." Booger-Face pinches his nose between his fingers. "The smell gets me every time."

Booger-Face speaks truth. There's nothing like a game of domino barfing.

"Give me your shoe!"

Dog Boy must be crazy. What's he wanna puke in

my shoe for?

"Now!" He dives on me, his hands scrambling for my foot.

The dress shoe pops off easy, and in one swift move he flings it out the open window.

"Whatcha go and do that for?"

"They've got the other one."

"So? Now I ain't got either of them." I still don't know how I'm gonna explain this dress-shoe mishap to the theater department. I'm probably gonna owe someone some money.

"They're using the smell from your shoe to track us." He snarls, and his creepy eyes glow green.

"Whoa." Booger-Face flattens himself against the car door, as far from Dog Boy as he can get. "What's with your eyes?"

"My eyes are fine. And so are my ears. They still have his scent. Stop the car. There's a creek over there."

The four of us stare at him. If Gene's eyes weren't on the road, he'd be turned around in his seat and staring too. How'd this kid know there's a creek? Even I don't know there's a creek, and I live in this town.

"Stop. Now." Dog Boy locks eyes with Finley. "I'm trying to save your brother. I'm trying to save you all."

"How do you know I'm his brother?" Dog Boy must have ESP. That's how he knows so much.

"You smell related."

Now I'm really creeped out.

"Gene, would you please pull over?" Finley says over the sounds of wind and road.

The car eases to the shoulder and stops.

"Only fifteen minutes to the manor. What're we stopping for, boys?"

"I think this kid wants to pee in the creek or something," Booger-Face says.

Dog Boy points at me. "You. Come. The rest of you, stay." He throws open the door and leaps out.

The overhead light blasts my eyes. "I'm not leaving Finley if you think people are after us."

"I'll be fine. Go with him."

Gene twists in the front seat and pops open the glove box. He hands me a flashlight. "Ten minutes. Then I'll be the one to come after you."

Reluctantly, I leave my brother and follow Dog Boy. The flashlight jiggles in my hand, bouncing light down a hill, casting shadows against the trees. A low fog hugs the ground, and the crickets are having a jamboree tonight. Dog Boy's back disappears and reappears. He's crouched like he's running on all fours. Sticks and rocks poke through my socks as I try to keep up.

Dog Boy shows up next to me, grabs my arm, and pulls me along.

Water bubbles against rocks beyond the tree line. The ground is soft and wet beneath my shoeless feet. When we get to the creek bank, I slip and land splat on my backside with an *oomph*!

Hands reach for me to help me back up . . . but, no, they are definitely not helping me back up. Dog Boy yanks off one of my socks and tosses it high into a tree.

Before I can say, "Hey, I gotta give that back to the theater department," he's ripped my shirt sleeves off at the seams and flung them into the creek.

My bare elbow sinks into the mud when I turn to my side. I shine the flashlight on the water and watch the fabric twist like silver fish in the current. "You're nuts, you know that?"

"Sit up." He grabs my tie at the knot and tears it into three pieces. One . . . after . . . the other, tie parts join the shirt sleeves.

"How?" He's shredding fabric like it's tissue paper.

And he's not done with me yet. The now-sleeveless shirt that I'm still wearing gets split up the back and torn off me like an orange peel. Yep. Into the creek it goes.

I take my other sock off myself and hand it over. I'm not a total dufus. I get where he's going with this. By getting rid of my clothes, he's cutting off the trail, or at least making it harder to track me. But there's one exception.

"The pants stay." I hike them up so he knows I mean business.

"Fine. Roll."

Come. Stay. Sit. Roll. What's next with this kid? Play dead?

Smack. Something cold and wet slides down my chin.

Smack. Splat. Thwump. More wet.

"Hey!"

Sploosh! Ugh, that one got me right in the mouth. Grit and slime coat my teeth and tongue. The kid's throwing mud at me.

"It would be easier," he says, "if you rolled."

❖ ❖ ❖

I scramble up the hill after Dog Boy. Drying mud cracks on my skin. My elbows and knees tighten when I bend them. I try not to inhale too deeply. I don't wanna suck mud up my nose.

"That you, Mick?"

"Coming, Gene."

"What the−?"

I squint against the beam from a second flashlight.

"Kids." Gene *tsks* at me. "Just get in." He douses the light and we climb back into the sedan.

Booger-Face gives me the once-over before I shut the car door behind me. "Did ya' fall in?"

"Sorta. We had to kill my scent."

"Looks like you killed something, all right."

"My father's gonna kill *me*. You're getting mud all over the—"

"Leather upholstery. I know."

"Will this stop them from following us?" Finley fidgets.

"For a little while." Dog Boy stares out the window again as Gene steers us off the shoulder. "But they'll pick up the scent again. They always do."

"Why do they want Mick so bad?" Booger-Face pokes my arm, and dried mud flakes onto the seat. "Shouldn't they be sniffing you out, instead?"

"I have a common scent, like any other dog. The rest of you, your stink's unique." Finley gives me a whiff, then smells his own armpit and crinkles his nose. Dog Boy shakes his head and continues. "They're following Mick's trail to get to me."

"Then why do they want *you* so bad? Why they have you locked in a cage, anyway?" Booger-Face pokes me again. This time a whole clod drops off, and PJ sighs.

"They want my secret."

"Secret? What kinda secret?" I'm not sure I wanna know, but sometimes my mouth asks the question before my brain tells me to shut up.

Dog Boy looks at each of us in turn. "Once we get someplace safe, I'll show you."

Hang Out with a Werewolf

"CAN I TAKE A SHOWER NOW?" We stand in the middle of PJ's entrance hall. The wooden peacock engraved in the floor looks like he's gonna peck at me if I track any more mud into this house. Even PJ's cat, Mittens, hisses at us before darting up the stairs.

"The answer to that question is a definite yes." Nanny Vargas crosses her arms and purses her lips at me. I wonder if she's part peacock. She definitely rules the roost when PJ's parents are out of town. Maybe when they're in town, too. "There's a shower in the mudroom we use for the pets. Past the kitchen. Make a left. "And you"—she points at Dog Boy—"I'll take you to wash up in PJ's bathroom. You can wear some of his clothes while I clean and mend those."

Perfect. *I'm* the one who gets the animal shower.

I can't decide if walking slow or fast releases more dried mud, so I kinda do both and skip-hop-slide to the back of the manor.

PJ's mudroom has never actually seen mud. It's hospital clean except for my contamination. I scrape off the pants I borrowed from the theater department. Creek gook got all the way through to my underwear. I throw the pants into the sink and my underwear into a trash can. Mom will think I went mud wrestling instead of to the circus. Might as well toss them.

The water warms my skin, and whatever soap Nanny Vargas uses on their pets reeks like overripe berries. Before long, I end up smelling like mom's hot fruit crumble, and my stomach grumbles about myself to myself, 'cause there's nothing better than my mom's cooking. Takes forever to scrub the muck outta my hair. When the last of the creek bed drains away, I wrap up in a towel big enough to go 'round me twice and then step out of the shower.

While the water was running, someone snatched the theater pants outta the sink and brought clean clothes, stacking them by the door. They're PJ's for sure. Only he believes a pink-flowered polo shirt works on a twelve-year-old guy. At least the underwear's normal.

As I head down the hallway toward the kitchen, the smells of oil, batter, and sweet maple drift toward me. There's a lot of clamoring and voices cheering up ahead.

"Go! Go! Go!"

The guys have their backs to me. They're hunkered around PJ's kitchen table like they're watching arm wrestling or a frog race or . . . an eating contest?

Booger-Face sits on one side of the table, facing Dog Boy on the other side. Piled in the center on a platter that could hold a forty-pound turkey is a mound of pancakes. Some of them got blueberries, some got pecans, and some got chocolate. Not the little choco-morsels either, but broken-chunks-of-chocolate-bar chocolate.

The same chocolate smears across the cheeks of both Booger-Face and Dog Boy. Chewed pancake bits spew as they stuff their faces.

"Go! Go! Go!"

The whole thing's kinda disgusting and kinda fascinating at the same time. Booger-Face is the Beach-wood Summer Fair Hot Dog Eating Champion and the Beaufort County Autumn Festival Pie Eating Champion in his age division two years running. But it looks like Dog Boy is giving him a run for his money. Yep, there is money on the table—at least five bucks—which half explains the enthusiasm.

Watching makes me hungry. I go to grab for a golden-brown pancake, but Dog Boy swipes my hand aside and growls at me. He *growls* at me!

"Pull up a seat over here, Mick. I made a couple for you before I ran out of eggs." Nanny Vargas closes a dishwasher loaded with dirty bowls and spatulas and turns to scrape off the griddle covering half of a six-burner stove. Her plump face is pink with effort, but a smile dances in her dark eyes. "Would you believe my arms are tired? Never made so many pancakes at once in my whole life, and I grew up in a house with five brothers and three sisters."

I climb onto a stool at the counter. A plate of three banana pancakes dusted with powdered sugar stare up at me.

"Syrup?" Nanny hands me a bottle shaped like a maple leaf. "You know, I'm usually asleep this time of night, but you boys are so wound up, I thought the carbs would settle you down."

"Thanks, Nanny Vargas. These are delicious!" Although when I say it, it sounds more like, "Fanx, Manny Agash. *Mumble mumble* uh-IF-ish!"

She pats my back and then returns to cleaning the griddle.

Booger-Face moans and clutches his distended belly. "I give. I'm gonna bust." He pushes away from the table. "I eat one more bite, I die." He moans again. "I explode, and *then* I die."

Dog Boy snatches the last two pancakes. "More for me." He stuffs them both into his mouth and gulps them whole. Two seconds later he opens his mouth again and releases—

"Aaaaaaaaaaaaaaarrrrrrrrrrrrrrrrrgggggggggggggg aaaaaaaaaaaahhhhhhhhh!"

—the world's longest, and loudest, belch. I mean it. This belch is record-breaking impressive. The sign over Dog Boy's cage at the circus should've said Belch Boy. Even Nanny's eyes widen and her jaw drops.

"That was awesome!" Finley laughs and claps.

I swallow my baby burp behind my hand. No way am I competing.

Gene enters the room and places his hand on Dog Boy's shoulder. "Got your parents on the phone. I'm sure you want to talk with them. PJ and the rest of you boys need to go to bed. It's after midnight. I made up the den for you. Got a fire going to cut the chill. Move 'em out."

He doesn't have to tell us again. Rescuing Dog Boy was exhausting, and I've got just enough energy to hear his story before I drop off. Nanny's efforts paid off. Pancakes in the middle of the night do make you sleepy. I guzzle the last of my milk, put my plate, glass, and fork in the sink, and trail behind the gang, while

Dog Boy leaves with Gene to talk to his parents on the phone.

We pass through PJ's ginormous dining room. The table's so long, if you're sitting at the head you'd need a bullhorn to talk to the person at the foot. Maybe PJ's parents use carrier pigeons like Mrs. Shumaker told us the US Army did in World War II. Crystal, china, and silver are stacked on a large piece of furniture. Looks like Nanny Vargas is staging a banquet for the Vanderbilts.

"Don't touch anything," Finley whispers to Booger-Face, his hands tucked into his pockets.

"I'm not breathing, either," Booger-Face whispers back.

PJ looks over his shoulder at me. "Dad's having a business dinner Monday night. Takes Nanny all weekend to get ready for it." He rolls his eyes. "I know, I know. He goes overboard. About everything. The string quartet goes up there." He points at a balcony above I didn't see earlier 'cause the chandelier was in the way.

"PJ, you need to spend the night at my house and see how the rest of us live."

"I'd like that, Mick," he says, surprising my snarky response right back into my mouth. PJ has a way of reminding me why we became friends: deep down below his awful taste in clothes and his Richie Rich upbringing, he's Mr. Nice Guy.

"The den is up ahead." PJ points at a columned archway.

Of course the den is more like *The Den* that opens off *The Library*. There are so many books it even smells like books. They're lined in shelves up to the ceiling, with a ladder on wheels so you can get to the books at the tippy top.

The Den has a stone fireplace large enough to roast a family of five. No sleeping bags are tossed around the floor for us. No siree—instead, there's a cot for each of us, made up with pillows, sheets, and thick fuzzy blankets.

Dog Boy surprises me when he darts from nowhere into the room and claims a cot by the fire. Now that he's in plain sight, I see he's wearing some of PJ's clothes too. They're much too big for him, but they're normal colored, meaning *not pink*. He cleaned up pretty well—mud and smudges gone—but without Nanny's pancakes masking his dog odor, the stink surrounds him like a cloud.

"Wow, PJ. This sure is nice." Finley sits on the cot next to Dog Boy. "Comfy, too." He fluffs the pillow, which squishes. Filled with goose feathers for sure.

Booger-Face takes the cot across from Dog Boy. PJ points at the cot in the center for me, and he plops on the one farthest from the fire. We sit in silence for what seems like hours, hypnotized by the crackling flames, zoning to our own thoughts. Booger-Face snores a little—he fell asleep with his eyes open.

I'm mostly watching Dog Boy. The shadows play hide-and-seek across his face, twisting his features. While I stare, his ears stretch into points and his nose distends. His cheeks hollow out, lips get thin and tight, and—jeez, his green eyes are glowing red now. Then the flames shift, and he's just a kid who needs a haircut.

My guts get squirmy again. I gotta know what's up with this kid. Booger-Face startles awake, and PJ jumps when my voice breaks the silence. "Why were you in a cage?"

My question yanks a cork out of a bottle.

"Why are those circus people after you?"

"You said they could smell Mick but not you. You said *you* . . . can smell *them*?"

"Where are your parents? Why aren't you with them?"

"What's your name?"

That last one came from Finley. Obviously it's the best question to ask first, and yeah, I'm simultaneously ashamed at myself and proud of my brother for thinking on my behalf.

"Padraig."

Booger-Face laughs. "Paws Dig?"

"No. Paw-*drig*. It's what my mom and dad call me. What my friends back home call me. Not Paws Dig. Not Dog Boy." His head whips around to glare at each of us.

He turns on Booger-Face, who's still chuckling. "You're the one they keep calling Booger-Face. That can't be your real name. Why do you let them call you that?"

Booger-Face sits up taller. "It's the name I chose. I gave it to myself. I don't *let* people call me Booger-Face. I *tell* them to call me Booger-Face."

Dog Boy's—I mean Padraig's—eyebrows knot together. "But why? Why would you choose to be insulted?"

"'Cause it's not an insult." I lean toward Booger-Face and I give him the look that says, *Time to fess up*.

He gives me the look back that says, *Yeah, OK*.

Maybe if Booger-Face shares his story, Padraig's will come right after.

Turning to Padraig, I tell him, "It's not an insult because it's his superpower."

Padraig frowns. "Is that a joke?"

"Show him, Booger-Face. Show him your super-power." Finley bounces on his cot like he's suddenly aged backward.

"What? What are you going to do?" PJ's eyes are huge in his head.

Booger-Face rises and crosses the room. He stands about twenty feet away and faces us.

"Oh, this is gonna be good." Finley holds on to the sides of his cot.

"You better clear a path. I'm gonna aim for the fireplace." Booger-Face stretches his arms to the side and wiggles his fingertips in preparation.

We scoot the cots out of the way, and I stand back a little. I've never seen him use a fireplace before. The last time he did this in front of me, his target was a drinking fountain at the opposite end of the school hallway. Finley's only heard my stories. Now he gets to see it for himself.

PJ and Padraig are clueless. In fact, PJ suddenly steps in front of the fireplace with his hands up. "You're not gonna break anything are you?"

"Move outta the way, PJ, or you'll never be the same," I tell him.

His mouth falls open and he ducks behind Finley.

"Here goes."

The sound is what gets to you first. A low, wet rumble as Booger-Face draws air through his mouth and nose. Then, like a train closing in, the rumble morphs into a roar. Booger-Face places his hand alongside his nose as the pressure builds. He arches his neck, flares his nostrils open, and . . . a gallon-sized snot rocket blasts across the room and splats onto the fire, completely smothering the flames and pitching us into darkness.

"Someone get the lights."

They flash on and I squint for a second.

"Whoa. What is this stuff?" PJ prods the fireplace logs with an iron poker.

Gooey, transparent mucus oozes off the logs and sizzles when it hits the hot coals.

"Boogers. Super boogers." Booger-Face rubs his nose and sniffles.

Padraig extends his hand to shake Booger-Face's. "That was epic."

"You rock, Booger-Face," Finley cheers. "A phlegm torpedo! A mucus cannonball! Do it again!"

"Naw, takes me all day to build to that level."

"You know, if you eat and drink a lot of dairy, you could probably energize faster." PJ tries to get the fire going again with a super-long lighter and a handful of fresh kindling. "What?" He looks at everyone staring at him. "It's a known fact dairy is an inflammatory and makes mucus in the body. It's why I never drink milk before I perform with the Singing Knights at my school."

"Remind me never to play Useless Trivia with you." I push the cots back into place. "And please don't sing." I imagine PJ's voice is high-pitched, girly, and disturbing.

"Don't worry. I only sing with my group. Looks like the wood isn't going to burn now. We're done with the fire for tonight." PJ puts the lighter in a box and tucks it on a shelf. "Your boogers are a good fire retardant."

"That's for the best. It's better for me to show you *my* superpower with all the lamps on. It can be scary by firelight." Padraig gestures at the cots. "You better sit for this. I'm going to show you why Auguste Linville and the Purnima brothers kidnapped me from my parents, why they keep me locked in a cage, and why I have such a keen sense of hearing and smell. I need a blanket. Toss me one?"

I throw him mine, and he pins the edges close around himself with one hand while his other hand disappears underneath. Not sure what he's up to until I see PJ's clothes drop at his feet.

"You naked under there?" Booger-Face asks.

"Yeah. Don't want to ruin these nice clothes."

I stand by Finley, 'cause when things get weird we gotta stick together, and the strange, green-eyed boy we rescued from a cage at the circus—who is now naked and wrapped in a blanket in PJ's den—definitely falls into the category "weird."

He shivers like he's suddenly standing in Siberia, and then he starts to pant. Rapid, shallow breaths and then deep, hungry gulps of air. In front of my eyes, his skin starts to mottle like an oil spill on asphalt, yellow and gray, orange and brown. His nose and lips turn black.

"Is that hair?" Finley grabs my arm. He's giving me bruises tonight. "On his face? Real hair?"

At first it's a five-o'clock shadow, same as Uncle George gets, but it spreads quick and thickens into a shaggy coat of fur covering his face and neck. Banana pancakes gurgle in my stomach.

The thing that once was Padraig shakes its head. Its face is no longer a face. It's a snout. A pink tongue lolls between sharp, white teeth. Leathery nostrils twitch and flare. Enlarged, pointy, fur-lined ears pivot. The eyes . . . the eyes glow green, lit from within.

It crouches onto its four clawed paws, shakes off the blanket, and curls its thick tail on the floor as it sits on its haunches. Throwing its head back, nose stretched to the ceiling, it . . . howls.

STEP 8

Learn a Few Things

"QUICK. TURN OFF the lights. Hide. Nanny's coming."
PJ pulls his head back into the room and carefully
shuts the door with a tiny click.

The wolf cub pounces on Padraig's cot, and Booger-
Face throws a blanket over him. I swipe at the light
switch, and the humans in the room assume sleeping
positions just as Nanny cracks open the door.

"Boys?" She waits a moment for a response.

Booger-Face fakes a soft snore, and it takes all my
willpower not to give him a kick. But Nanny buys it.
We wait as her slippered feet shuffle away, and then
we wait some more just in case.

PJ turns on a lamp sitting on a side table. "That was
close. Is he OK?"

The blanketed lump on Padraig's cot's immobile.
I pinch a corner of the cover and peel it back.

The kid-turned-wolf who's a boy again lifts his head. "Can I have those clothes back?"

Finley retrieves the pile and hands it over to Padraig. PJ and I hold up the blanket with our backs turned so the kid can have some privacy, while Booger-Face sits dazed as a bird that fell out of a tree.

"Well now we know why they called him Dog Boy."

Padraig comes around and stands by the fireplace. Boogers still glisten on the blackened wood. "I know everyone's tired and wants to go to bed, but if you can stay awake a little longer, I'd like to tell you my story."

"You better tell us, 'cause I don't think I'll ever sleep again until you do."

Booger-Face is right. My adrenaline can easily keep me going like a hamster guzzling Mountain Dew on an exercise wheel.

Finley's turned into a bobblehead doll. "But keep the lights on."

Padraig has our full attention. Suddenly he looks and sounds older than eight, if that's even his real age. "My parents are descendants of the Fáelad from Ireland. They moved to Canada to escape persecution. That's where I was born. Canada. We're lycanthropes. Shape-changers. The Wolven. We can change our form into a wolf whenever we want."

"Wow. So you don't need the moon?" Booger-Face

says exactly what I'm thinking. All the werewolf stories I've ever heard include a curse and a full moon.

"Nope. No moon. The wolf is a part of my DNA. I control the wolf as easy as I control my legs when I want to walk across the room. That's what makes my family and me different from the Purnima brothers. They wish they could control their transformation, but they can't. Their wolf is ruled by the lunar cycle."

"The Purnima brothers are werewolves too?" Why didn't I see it before? It all falls into place now: the growling, the teeth, the tracking. "Finley, you were right. You said those clowns were like Wolverine, and we shrugged you off."

Finley's face pinks. "It's OK. I'm used to it."

I shrink to about two inches tall. I shoulda stood up for him when I had the chance. Now I gotta make this up to him somehow.

He turns his attention to Padraig. "Do you super heal? Like they do?"

"Yes. But I don't purposefully hurt myself like they do. They're always testing how far they can go. It's why Mr. Linville wants them for his circus."

"I still don't get what they want you for." Booger-Face keeps staring at Padraig like he's gonna turn all wolf cub again.

"My blood. Mr. Linville's been taking my blood and

giving it to the Purnima brothers to try to change them with it. He wants them to become wolves no matter what shape the moon's in."

"Does your blood work on them?" I don't want to know how they get Padraig's blood. Inject it? Drink it? Bathe in it? Triple gross.

"It kinda helps. Temporarily. Gives them some wolf powers while they still look human. But it wears off. That's why they'll never let me go. They need me."

"So how come they can't do what you do on their own?"

"They were bit and I was born."

Booger-Face gets up and starts to pace. "This is some messed-up stuff. Not only do werewolves exist, but there are two kinds."

Me and Finley give each other our nothing-sur-prises-us-anymore look. After pirate zombies, creepy mermaids, and robot bugs, a pack of circus werewolves is just another day in Beachwood.

"Technically, I'm not a werewolf. I'm a lycanthrope. Werewolves become werewolves from a virus in saliva. It's spread from biting. If you don't get eaten and survive the bite, you become a werewolf."

"That's what you meant when you said, 'If they catch you, they'll eat you.'"

Padraig nods.

The lump in my throat lodges there, refusing to move no matter how hard I swallow. "Do you? Eat people?"

"Of course not. And I don't bite people, either. And even if I did bite you, my saliva wouldn't turn you. I don't have the virus. I don't make others of my kind that way."

I don't need the details about how he does make little werewolves, so I ask a more pressing question. "What keeps the Purnima brothers from tracking you? Can't they follow you back to Canada and kidnap you again?"

"As long as I'm in human form, I smell like an ordinary dog. Once I'm in wolf form, they can hunt me like anybody else." He bows his head. "I took a big risk just now, turning for you guys. Maybe once I'm reunited with my family we'll have to move to another country. Somewhere the Purnima brothers won't follow us."

"Like China."

"Yeah. Like China."

"When are your parents gonna get here?" PJ, who's been awful quiet up to now, seems eager to be rid of our new friend. Can't say I blame him. Not sure I'd want some strange kid hiding out from a pack of werewolves at my house.

"They said they couldn't get a flight into Coastal

Carolina Airport until tomorrow night."

Booger-Face throws his hands into the air. "Tomorrow night? How're we gonna keep you safe until tomorrow night? Those clowns were already tracking us using Mick's shoe. They probably got a whiff of you when you changed into a werewolf in front of us. They could have the place surrounded right now!" He scans the room as if the Purnima brothers are hiding in the shadows, biding their time, ready to pounce.

"Calm down," Finley says, sounding a lot like Mom. "We're doing great. Padraig made them lose the scent at the creek. Tonight's almost over. We just have to worry about all day tomorrow."

"We should have a plan. Mick and Finley come up with great plans. Don't you, Mick? Finley?" PJ says.

"That's right. They do. Whatcha got this time?"

Nice to know PJ and Booger-Face have confidence in the Bogerman brothers. Finley shrugs and I scrub my hair with my hand. Whatever they think we're capable of, I'm not feeling very capable right now. The only plan I've got is to take cover and hide. "You got a basement, PJ? A bomb shelter?"

"No. And no. Sorry."

"Then I got nothing." I don't even ask Finley if he's got something up his sleeve. The look on his face says he's tapped out of werewolf-avoidance ideas.

Vmmm. Vmmm. Booger-Face's phone starts vibrating across the table and makes me jump two feet off the cot.

"Who's texting so late? It's gotta be like 4:00 in the morning."

It vibrates again, rattling against the wood. I know why Booger-Face doesn't want to look and see who it is. There's only two things that reach out after 10:00 p.m.: parents and trouble.

"Want me to look?" I ask.

"No. I got it." Booger-Face rises and grabs his cell just as it starts vibrating again. He reads the messages and his mouth drops open so wide Gene could drive the sedan up his tongue and park behind his tonsils.

Before I can finish saying, "What? What is it? Who is it?" Booger-Face's phone lies in my outstretched hand. There are three texts. All from Neill Gillis.

Those clowns are werewolves.

They followed us to Brendan's house.

One of them bit Cooper.

STEP 9

Try Not to Panic

"OH NO! THIS IS BAD."

"How'd they find Neill and Cooper?"

"What're we gonna do?"

"Will Cooper be a werewolf now?"

"What will his parents think? He's gonna have to get homeschooled for sure."

"Will they put him in a cage at the circus?"

"Hold it! Everyone, stop!" Padraig's voice is nearly a howl cutting through the clamor.

We all fall silent, listening to each other breathe.

Finally, Finley says, "You should text him back and find out if the Purnima brothers are still there."

Aw, man. That one thought is worse than all the thoughts that came before it.

"Go ahead." Booger-Face points to the phone. "Text him."

Me? How'd I become the designated texter? My thumbs move slow and steady: *Are the Purnima brothers with you now?*

Yes, we are.

Booger-Face's phone slips from my slick hands and thuds onto the rug.

"What did Neill say?" PJ is five shades whiter than Nanny Vargas's dining room tablecloth.

Finley recovers the phone at my feet. "It's not Neill who texted back. It's one of *them*."

"Let me see."

Finley shows Padraig the screen.

"Ask them what they want, but I'm sure what they're going to say."

Finley types the question while we all huddle around him. *What do you want?*

Give us the boy and we won't bite anyone else. Give us the boy and we won't eat your friends.

"Now what?" he says when he's done reading the message to us. He hands the phone back to Booger-Face.

"I'll go back to the Purnima brothers. We'll make a trade. Me for your friends. I'd like to write a letter to my parents. Will you give it to them?"

"Jeez. We can't do that." Finley looks at me with his little kid-brother eyes like he suddenly needs a big brother. "There's gotta be another way."

"Whatever we do, we have to do it before tomorrow night." PJ's got his own phone out now, thumbing through a bunch of screens.

"Why? What's so special about tomorrow night besides Padraig's parents are flying in from Canada?"

PJ shows me the weather website he's pulled up on his phone. "There's gonna be a full moon. The Purnima brothers will be real werewolves."

"Can this get any worse?"

"Yes. Yes it can." Padraig's eyes flash green. "You ever hear about New City Village in New Jersey? The town where everyone disappeared in 1992?"

In unison, the four of us shake our heads at him.

"Werewolves. Took out the whole town. Men. Women. Kids. Everyone. They call it Demon Alley now."

PJ's thumbs are on his phone again. "Wow, he's right. The Internet says there really is a Demon Alley."

"Great. Now we gotta worry about the whole neighborhood?" Booger-Face starts typing search terms into his phone: werewolves, full moon, bites.

"Let's stick to worrying about Cooper, Neill, and Brendan and his family. We gotta tell the Purnima brothers something. We need to stall them. Make them think we're giving them what they want to buy us some time." It's the only idea I can come up with. At least it's something.

Padraig grabs PJ's phone and starts texting. His thumbs move fast, like the screen is too hot to touch for very long. He hands it to me when he's done.

"He told them we'll be there in a few hours. That we need a chance to sneak away and arrange transportation."

"I got it!" Booger-Face holds up his phone. "Garlic."

"Garlic's for vampires. We need silver bullets."

Padraig smiles at Finley. "You're half right. Silver is the cure, but it doesn't have to be bullets. As long as any kind of silver touches their blood, they change back to human forever. Or you can take out the alpha. If the alpha dies, the entire bloodline goes back to normal. Everyone he's ever bitten and everyone they've ever bitten. The whole infected bloodline."

"Who's the alpha?" That seems to be the most direct route. Set a trap for the alpha, and then the Purnima brothers go from circus werewolves to just . . . clowns.

"Don't know. I heard the brothers talking. They said Frido got bit first by some guy at a diner ten years ago. Haven't seen the guy since. They think he's the alpha."

"Good luck finding him." Booger-Face punches his fist into his hand. "Looks like we gotta silverize the Purnima brothers one by one."

"And how exactly are we supposed to do that?" A good plan's gotta have details; otherwise, it's what

Uncle George calls "marshmallow fluff."

"I've got silver. Lots of it. Come look." PJ leads us back into the dining room. When he turns on the lights, Nanny's pile of silverware gleams.

"How're we gonna use this stuff? Trip Frido so he scrapes a knee, and then rub a spoon on his wound?" The idea of silverizing the Purnima brothers is looking grim.

"We could use the knives," Finley offers.

"Only the handles are silver. The stabby part is stainless steel." PJ holds up one of the knives so we can see the difference.

I wouldn't know stainless from tin. It all looks shiny to me.

"We could melt them down. Mold them into spearheads."

"Got an industrial-grade crucible and a blowtorch, PJ?" Savannah's showed me how to melt down metal before. It's no easy task. She wears a blacksmith apron, welding mask, the works. I kinda wish she were here instead of in China. Her big brain would've had a solution to our troubles in no time. Or Uncle George. He's resourceful.

"No. I don't have that kinda stuff. But I think the forks are pointy enough. Maybe we can use them."

The forks! My mind churns like the waves crashing

against Cutter's Crag. "Duct tape. Long handles like the ones on brooms and mops. You got a work bench we can use?"

"There's one in the garage."

"Bring the silver. Gather up the rest of the supplies. I'll meet you there. Booger-Face, can I borrow your phone? I'm gonna call in a favor."

STEP 10

Call In a Favor

WHEN I MEET UP with the guys, the sky is pale gray. Night came and went and I didn't sleep. It's crazy, but I don't even feel tired anymore, like my brain shifted into overdrive and my body's tagging along for the ride.

"So what's the plan, Mick?" Booger-Face sets a spear on top of a stack of more spears propped against the wall. An acre of duct tape straps Nanny's silverware to the narrow poles. They look like appetizer forks for giants.

Everyone looks at me all hopeful, like I have all the answers. I can't bear to tell 'em I'm winging this. Fortunately, if I talk like I know what I'm talking about, I make us all feel confident.

"Uncle George is on his way. He can fit two of us in his cab: Finley and Padraig—they're the youngest.

The rest of us will have to get to Brendan's house some other way."

"What about Gene?" Finley offers.

PJ shakes his head. "He has the weekend off. He left last night."

"Nanny?"

"Definitely no. We gotta be gone before she notices we snagged the silver." Nanny Vargas is a speed demon in a golf cart. The moment she finds only butter knives on her buffet table, she'll catch us in no time and probably make us repolish every piece.

PJ raises his hand. "I have scooters."

"What? Like Razors?"

"No. Yamaha Vino Classics. Got them for Christmas. One's mine and the other one's my sister's. She won't mind if you ride it. She's at our place in Belize with my mom for spring break."

"I thought your place was in Barcelona."

"We have one there too. I know. Most people don't have property all over the world."

"Sometimes Mick and I pretend the shed's the international space station," Finley shares with everyone before I can kick him.

I give him the evil eye instead. "Let's see those scooters."

PJ takes us around to the side of the garage nearest

the rec room. Looks like two of Mr. Williams's cars are missing today. There's usually five parked in here. The scooters line up against the wall: one blue with PJ's name in green flames, and one pink with Daphne's name in purple flowers. I already know how this is gonna go, but I try to head it off anyway.

"I'll take the blue one."

"That's mine," PJ says. "My sister won't let me ride hers anyway." He purses his lips like a fish. "What? She didn't say *you* couldn't."

"Booger-Face? What about you?" Maybe he'll take one for the team.

"I can't drive. I'll just ride on the back of PJ's."

UGH!

Booger-Face's phone chimes in my pocket. "It's my Uncle George. He needs someone to open the gate."

❖ ❖ ❖

If you didn't know Uncle George and you saw him for the first time, you'd think he drove a Harley Davidson instead of a delivery truck. He's got a head of black shaggy hair, always needs a shave, likes to wear a leather vest with chains across the pocket and a pair of dusty cowboy boots, and he's got a wicked skull with fire eyes sneering from his bicep.

When he climbs down from the cab of his truck, PJ ducks behind Booger-Face and says, "Your uncle's kind of scary."

"Wait till he smiles. It'll bust his image," I reassure him.

Uncle George strides up to me with arms wide. "Mick!" He grins, and suddenly his stern face morphs into Disney's Goofy. Booger-Face laughs, and Uncle George laughs right along with him.

He bends down to squeeze me, then scoops up Finley and squeezes us together. "Missed you two. Introduce me to your friends."

"Guys, this is my Uncle George, my Mom's brother. Uncle George, you know Booger-Face. That's PJ Williams behind him. It's his house. And this over here is Padraig. He's the one I told you about on the phone."

Uncle George scans Padraig and then narrows his eyes. "You will *not* rejoin the Purnima brothers. I'm going to have a few words with them, and you're going to stay with Finley in my truck until it's safe to come out. Understand?"

Padraig nods.

"Good. Finley, go grab Mick's and your presents. Boys, let's take a look at these weapons of yours."

"He knows the Purnima brothers are werewolves, right?" PJ whispers to me from behind his hand.

"Yeah. He's not like most adults. He's cool."

"That's for sure."

Uncle George examines the stack of fork-spears. Every broom and mop handle in PJ's mansion has been repurposed. "A fine arsenal. Have you practiced using them?"

PJ shrugs. "We didn't get that far."

Before you can say, "Stack those sandbags from the garage onto the driveway," we've got three three-foot piles and Uncle George is supervising Booger-Face's one-handed thrust. "Make sure you hit 'em hard enough to puncture the skin, but avoid the face, torso . . . uh, the sensitive parts. You're trying to introduce silver into their bloodstream, not do any permanent damage. Unless we find the alpha. Then you let me deal with *him*. Understand?"

"Your uncle acts like he's done this before," Booger-Face says.

"Yeah. Well. He travels a lot."

That answer seems to satisfy Booger-Face, but his comment gnaws at me. How *does* Uncle George know so much about taking out werewolves?

Finley and Padraig half-carry, half-drag two large boxes up the driveway toward us.

"Is this what I think it is?" I gotta clamp my mouth to keep from giggling as I tear into the box with my name scrawled in marker across the top. Inside are a black bow and a half dozen arrows strapped together with a plastic tie. The fact that they have suction cup tips doesn't even faze me until Booger-Face snickers.

Uncle George saves the day. "I saw a grinding wheel in the garage. Booger-Face, how 'bout I show you how to turn one of those silver spoons into an arrowhead? But first, Finley needs to open his present."

"It's not another bow, is it?" I hope not. Twinkie presents lost their cool factor when I was five and he was three.

"Finley didn't ask for a bow."

Now I'm curious. It takes forever for Finley to get his box open. Then there's an acre of tissue paper to dive through. He finally pulls out a huge . . . boomerang?

"Thanks, Uncle George! It's just what I wanted."

Uncle George claps his hands. "All right, boys, let's get to work. Booger-Face, grab those spoons and come with me. Finley, why don't you show Padraig how to throw that boomerang? Mick, go ahead and practice using your bow on the sandbags. And PJ, you should deal with that angry woman charging over your lawn in a golf cart."

STEP 11

Practice Some Skills

SHOOTING SANDBAGS with a bow and suction cup arrows is harder than it sounds, especially when Nanny Vargas screams at PJ about her lost silverware while I'm trying to concentrate. I miss every . . . single . . . shot. I bet even if I stomp over and jam one of these idiot arrows into one of those stupid sandbags with my bare hands, all I'd hit would be air.

When PJ joins me, he looks like he's been in a windstorm.

"What happened to you?"

"Nanny Vargas."

"And?"

"She's not happy that we snagged my grandmother's silver. It's going to be hard to find replacements before the dinner party. She says she's going to call my parents and charge my trust fund."

"What'd you tell her we did with it?"

"The truth, of course. I told her we made the forks into spears and your uncle is showing Booger-Face how to turn spoons into arrowheads, and when she screamed, 'Why would you do such things?' I told her we're going to save Beachwood from circus werewolves."

Did I just miss the last stairstep? PJ told her the truth? "What did she say about the werewolves?"

"She told me I better come up with a better story for my parents or I'll spend the rest of my spring break polishing everything that shines in the house." A queasy look slides across his face. "We have a lot of shiny things in our house, Mick."

"We'll come up with a way to make it up to her."

"Hope so. Oh, and by the way, you're holding your bow like a dodo bird. May I?"

It's the "May I" uber-politeness that throws me off the fact PJ just insulted me with one of the most ridiculous insults I've ever heard. I hand off my bow and an arrow like a robot with new instructions. What's a dodo bird, anyway?

PJ holds the bow in his left hand and places his feet shoulder-width apart. He nocks the arrow, holding it so one of the vanes points outward. In one motion, he raises, draws, aims, and releases. The arrow glides through the air and lands in the sandbag stack farthest away. In fact, the arrow hits dead center with enough force the suction cup disappears inside the canvas and sand leaks out.

"How'd you learn to do that?"

"Competitive archery. Three years," he mumbles, staring at his feet.

Don't know why he's embarrassed. He's got real skills. "Teach me."

PJ lights up like the Fourth of July and hands my bow back. "Hold it like this." He helps me into position. "Nock the arrow here. That's good. Now breathe in when you draw back. Keep your elbow here. Release your breath and your arrow at the same time."

I do exactly as he says, and my arrow skids along the ground until it crashes into the bottom of the closest stack of sandbags. "I finally hit the target!"

"Um . . . yeah. You did."

Booger-Face interrupts my lesson with a box jingling in his outstretched hands. "Look what I made. I got to use a Dremel."

Inside are ten oddly shaped silver arrowheads. I hope ten is enough.

"We can put 'em on with this." He pulls a small bottle of Gorilla Super Glue from his pocket.

Takes us a few minutes to replace out the suction cups and put the glue in the right spots. PJ accidently glues his shoe to the driveway, and we end up leaving it there. Luckily he's got an extra pair nearby. When Uncle George joins us, Booger-Face shows him our finished weapons.

"Looks great. No, no." He flings up his palm when Booger-Face tries to give him an arrow. "You boys hang on to them. I made you this to carry them." He hands off a quiver made from two empty tennis ball containers duct taped together. Blue boat ropes act as straps so I can wear it on my back.

"Cool."

"How you doin' with the bow?" Uncle George looks so hopeful I hate to disappoint him.

"He's getting there," PJ says.

I'm about to thank PJ when Finley and Padraig trudge over the hill. Finley carries his boomerang across his shoulders. His narrowed eyes and scrunched nose tell me something's got him riled, and honestly, it takes a lot to get my brother mad. I'd know. I'm an expert brother-button-pusher.

Padraig's rubbing the back of his head and keeps giving Finley wary glances. Something went down between these two. Before I can ask, Finley says, "Padraig almost ate Sampson. I stopped him." He slaps the boomerang against his hand.

"Who's Sampson?" Uncle George asks.

"PJ's family has a pet peacock," Booger-Face tells him.

"Is Sampson OK? He loses his feathers when he's stressed. Does he have all his feathers?"

Finley calms PJ down. "He's great. He was splashing around in the fountain when we left."

"Listen, boys. We better get over to the Pipitones' house. It's almost 10:00 a.m., and we don't want to put your friends in any more risk."

Still rubbing his head, Padraig climbs into the truck cab, and Finley follows.

"We'll park down the block and walk to their house," Uncle George tells us before jumping into the driver's seat.

PJ wheels out each scooter. When I climb on to the pink one, PJ plops a helmet into my hands. "You have to wear one or you can get a ticket."

"If you post this on Instagram, I will roast Sampson with potatoes and carrots and serve him to Padraig myself." I take the purple helmet and strap it to my head. A white Pegasus with pink wings leaps over the top, a rainbow of sparkles shooting from its ... yeah, exactly.

Discover a Secret

BECAUSE IT'S A SATURDAY morning and the weather is perfect, and because thirty miles per hour is not fast enough to reduce my visibility to others, a total of eighteen people see me riding PJ's sister's scooter, wearing PJ's sister's helmet with my bow and quiver strapped to my back. I hope saving Beachwood from werewolves is worth destroying every ounce of my street cred.

We park by Uncle George's truck a couple blocks over at the edge of a cul-de-sac, and I resist the urge to fling the horrifying helmet of humiliation into the gutter. Finley and Padraig stay behind in the truck. Me, PJ, and Booger-Face follow Uncle George up the sidewalk to Brendan Pipitone's house.

"Stash the weapons in the bushes. PJ and Booger-Face, you stand guard outside. Mick, you come with me."

"Should we sneak through the basement window or break in through the back door?"

"Neither." Uncle George rings the doorbell.

Neill answers the door all wild-eyed and ghost pale. "Who are you?"

Uncle George steps aside so Neill can see me.

"Mick! This is all your fault. Cooper's a werewolf and you're to blame."

"Why don't we take this inside?" Uncle George grasps the door, and me and Neill slip inside.

All the shades are drawn. The house is cool and dark. The place smells funky, but familiar. "Where's Cooper?" I can't quite figure out how I know this smell. "Where's the clowns? How is this my fault?" Then it hits me— dog. The place smells like Bagel Boy, my neighbor's mutt, after he's rolled around at the dump in the middle of summer.

"Your stupid jacket."

I still don't understand.

Neill looks like he wants to strangle me. "The one you borrowed from school to get into the adults-only tent? The one you gave to Cooper right before we left? The one the werewolves used to track us?"

"Oh, that jacket." I forgot. I want to shrink into the carpet. Of course if werewolves can track a guy from his shoe, they can do it from his jacket. It is my fault.

"Where is he?"

"In the kitchen with the big, scary guy."

"Only one?"

"The others went to scope out the town."

"And the Pipitones? Brendan?"

"They're all tied up in the basement."

"Why aren't you tied up in the basement?"

"'Cause I get to answer the door."

"Well, let's go see the big, scary guy in the kitchen." Uncle George leads the way.

Neill whispers, "Didn't you bring that Dog Boy kid with you? He's not going to bargain without him."

"We'll see about that," Uncle George says over his shoulder.

My intestines tighten like they're gonna make a run for it and leave me gutless in the living room. After watching the Purnima brothers perform last night, seeing one up close and personal is not on my list of spring break treats. The hallway to the kitchen stretches into a tunnel.

Neill pokes me in the back, propelling me forward. In the kitchen, Cooper slumps in a chair, his head buried in his arms on the table like he's sleeping. At the head of the table, a gorilla-shaped man sneers when we enter the room. His gaze locks on to me and Uncle George, and even in the dim light I see recognition spread across the man's face.

"You!" he growls, standing.

The chair clatters to the floor and Cooper jolts awake. Thank goodness, it's still Cooper. He's sweaty and pale like he's fighting the flu, but his eyes don't glow green and his ears don't pivot. Unlike the circus werewolf, when he sees me, he doesn't know me.

"Cooper! Snap out of it."

He shakes his head and scrubs his face with his hands. "Mick?"

That's when I notice the hair on his knuckles. Did he always have hairy hands?

"Mick, get Cooper and Neill out of the house." Uncle George circles the table.

"I can't leave. Brendan and his parents are trapped downstairs." Neill takes Cooper's arm and I grab the other one.

"I'll keep them safe," Uncle George says without taking his eyes off Werewolf Man.

Me and Neill have to practically drag Cooper out of the kitchen. It's like he's half asleep. As we get him around the doorframe, I hear Werewolf Man snarl and say, "I never thought I'd see you again."

My feet sink in sudden quicksand. They know each other? I thought the Purnima brother recognized me from the circus, not Uncle George.

Pound. Smack. Crash.

"PJ and Booger-Face are outside," I yell at Neill when concern crosses his face. "Go. Take Cooper."

He hesitates. "What about you?"

"Just go."

Crack. Shatter.

Draping Cooper's arm over his shoulder, Neill shuffles to the front door.

I press against the wall outside the kitchen. My mind churns in a duel with my stomach. How does Uncle George know a circus werewolf?

"My brothers are gonna rip you apart."

Metal crashing and wood splintering vibrate through the walls, but it's the next thing I hear that tears my world in half.

"Once we get rid of you, this wolf nightmare will finally end. You ruined my life, and now you're gonna pay." The werewolf man lisps like he's got a fat lip or a swollen tongue, or both. But I heard his words, and he was saying them to my uncle.

I step into the doorway of the destroyed kitchen. Werewolf Man's pummeled face miraculously heals itself, thanks to Padraig's blood. I hardly pay attention. It's my uncle I see with new eyes.

"You're the alpha!" My words freeze the two werewolf men: the Purnima brother and my Uncle George.

"How could you?"

"Mick, it's not what you think."

My insides ache and my heart twists. It's hard to breathe, like I'm drowning on dry land. "You're a werewolf. And you bit him. And all his brothers. And they bit my friend. You're a monster."

"Mick, look out!"

Iron arms clamp around me. Hot breath coats my cheek. "Struggle and I'll snap you like a twig."

I don't have any fight left anyway. I'm a soggy noodle as Purnima brother two carries me across the kitchen, kicking broken furniture from his path. Before he lugs me to the basement, three brothers take down my uncle. He doesn't resist either.

Escape the Basement

MY LIPS STRADDLE A CLOTH that ties at the back of my head and traps my tongue on the floor of my mouth. Scratchy ropes link my hands behind my back. Cold seeps from the concrete into my legs.

Mr. and Mrs. Pipitone and Brendan stare at me, trying to communicate with nose wiggles, eyebrow twitches, and blinking. Even though they had all night and all morning to practice, they still don't have the hang of nonverbal face code.

I wish Finley was here. He knows one blink is yes and two is no. The more I think about it, everyone but Brendan and his parents know one blink is yes and two blinks is no.

While they're making faces, I scoot across the basement floor to the foot of the stairs. It's slow going, but I need to get as close to the Purnima brothers and my uncle as I can. I need to hear what they're talking about and try to wrap my head around the fact I'm related to a werewolf.

How long has he been one? I mean, as long as I've known him he's been a big, hairy guy who only hangs around with his sister when he's not making deliveries, but that doesn't make someone a werewolf. If it does, there's an awful lot of werewolves in the world. How'd he keep a secret like that from me? I'm his nephew. We're . . . we're . . . family.

Family sticks together.

Yes, he's a monster for what he's done, but that's not the uncle I know. The uncle I've known all my life is a good guy. He takes care of me and Finley and Mom. That's gotta count for something, right? Maybe it's like Jekyll and Hyde. When he's not a werewolf, he's cool Uncle George, and when he is a werewolf, his bad side comes out and he doesn't know what he's doing. Maybe if I can get my hands on one of those silver arrowheads from behind the bushes, I can fix him. I need to help him if I can.

With little hops, I push myself up the stairs, one . . . step . . . at a . . . time. My legs are wobbly. It's hard to be quiet. Dust swirls and I try not to sneeze. At the top, I press my ear against the door.

"Let's end this. Once he's out of the picture, we'll

all go back to normal. I want to be normal again. Not a stinking dog." It's the voice of the brother who was watching Cooper.

"Are you sure it's him? I remembered him bigger. Hairier."

"He was turned at the time, you idiot. I know it was him. I'll never forget his stench."

"Yeah, it was him, all right. Jumped us in the parking lot at the diner. The cook."

Something thuds to the kitchen floor, and I peer through the space under the door. My uncle's pressed to the ground with a boot.

"Hold up and think for a minute. If we lose our wolf blood, we lose our power. We lose our jobs."

"I like what I am."

"Me too. I've never felt more alive. Once Linville started giving us that dog kid's blood, I've been able to do things I never dreamed possible."

I count three pairs of work boots and a pair of gym shoes. There's at least four Purnima brothers that I can see. Where's the rest of them? There were six at the circus. Was it seven? Ugh. I can't remember. Finley would know.

"We need the boy. His blood helps control the wolf. His parents will come for him, and if we can get our hands on them ... Just think what their adult wolf blood could do for us. Let's not lose sight of our goal."

"Where's the boy? You were supposed to bring the boy!"

I close my eyes. I wish I could cover my ears.

"Stop it, Frido! We need to keep this alpha alive."

"Easy for you to say. You don't have a wife and kids. I don't want this anymore. I want to go back home. And this wolf is in my way!"

"No!"

"Ease up, brothers. Frido's always been the one who hates the wolf part of himself, but we're a pack. We need to stick together."

Through the sliver between the door and the floor, I watch hands pick Uncle George up by the scruff of the neck. He's dragged toward the door. The door I'm hiding behind! If the Purnima brothers see me snooping . . .

I flatten my body into a surfboard. If I slide down the stairs on my back, my tied hands will smack against the steps. If I slide on my stomach, it'll be my chin. Sideways bobsledding bops my hip and shoulder and lands me at the bottom in a squat. My uncle has an even worse time of it. After a couple brothers toss him, he winds up in a crumpled heap next to me.

While I was eavesdropping, Brendan and both his parents followed my lead and scooted themselves to the stairs. Now we circle Uncle George like he's the campfire and we're the Scouts getting ready to sing Kumbaya, except we can't 'cause we're tied up and gagged.

One Purnima brother casts a long shadow over our powwow. "If we don't find that boy by nightfall, we'll tear your town apart and everyone in it." He slams the door, leaving the five of us to imagine Beachwood over-run by werewolves.

Uncle George twists his fingers. His wrists are raw from the ropes. I'm sure mine look the same. They feel like I've been Wonder-Woman-blocking a herd of cats. Then I see what he's doing. Wiggling his index finger, he points down.

Mrs. Pipitone seems to understand. She twists her back to him and attempts to grab his right boot. She glances over her shoulder for confirmation, and Uncle George shakes his head. She goes for the left one, and now he nods. Her fingers slip as she tugs at the old leather. After a gazillion minutes, Uncle George's boot is two inches lower on his heel. Maybe she'll have it off by next week.

My uncle grunts twice, which I figure is another way to say no when your mouth is out of commission and you can't broadcast a couple blinks to an audience that ain't watching. Since Mrs. Pipitone keeps tugging on his boot, her understanding of secret code must be limited to hand signals.

I grunt too. She looks up at me and I shake my head at her. Finally she stops. An idea grabs hold of me, but Mrs. Pipitone's gonna have to move aside for me to try it out. I got no clue how to get her to move, so I hope she can take a hint. She can! 'Cause when I wiggle like a puppy, she rolls away to give me room. My feet replace her hands, and I grip my uncle's boot between my gym shoes.

He and I look like a couple forks in a box, him in front, me behind, but I'm able to bend my knees and get some momentum. With a couple grip-pushes, Uncle George's cowboy boot slides right off.

Strapped to his calf, a knife in a sheath waits to set us free.

And waits, and waits.

My eyes dart from face to face, and they all seem to say, "Now what?"

Except Brendan. The normal pinched panic on his face has been miraculously replaced with cool determination. He starts rubbing the heels of his shoes against the edge of the first step. He's wearing some goofy-looking, red canvas slip-ons with no laces and no socks, which ends up being exactly what we need.

Both his shoes clomp to the floor, revealing ten of

the longest toes I've ever seen, and darn if he doesn't grab the hilt of Uncle George's knife between a couple of those monkey toes and pull it right out like Excalibur from the stone. Brendan grins around the gag in his mouth, and I grin right back.

You are definitely the ape-king of Camelot, my friend.

He holds the knife tight with those super toes of his, and I scoot, scoot over next to him. Pressing the ropes binding my hands against the blade, sawing up and down, up and down, my wrists spring apart as the rope falls away.

After untying my gag and cutting apart my ankles, I work on getting Brendan free. He deserves to be first after his feet saved the day. Together we remove the gags from Mr. and Mrs. Pipitone and Uncle George, but with only one knife, cutting through all the ropes takes time.

Too much time.

I'm sure we've been at this for hours. Any moment a Purnima brother's gonna come down the stairs for a taste of one of us. Since Uncle George is already a werewolf, there's a one-in-four chance I'll be next.

But that's not what's got me shaking in my laced-up sneakers. Finley's out there with Padraig: sitting ducks in a truck with some keen-nosed werewolves on their trail. And what happened to PJ and Booger-Face guarding the front door? I scan the basement for something sharp while Brendan works on his dad's ropes.

"There's a pruning saw in the red toolbox behind the stairs," Mrs. Pipitone tells me. Sure enough, when I open the box, the saw lies right on top of the wrenches.

As I hack away at my Uncle's ropes, I use the opportunity to hit him with my questions. Until I free him, he's gotta stay put and listen.

"Why didn't you tell me?"

"I'm sorry. I didn't want to scare you. I was going to tell you when you got older."

"Is it why you only visit certain times? So we don't see you change? So you don't eat us for dinner when we have you over for dinner?"

He sighs. "Yeah."

"Does Mom know?"

"No. She doesn't. I was hoping we could keep it that way." He lays his hand on my shoulder as I work on freeing his feet. "Mick, look at me a sec."

I do what he asks 'cause he's my family, and when I look into his eyes, all I see is my Uncle George. No werewolf in disguise.

"I'm not the alpha. I swear to you, I'm not. But if the Purnima brothers think that I am, well, it can help me help you and your friends."

"But you bit them. You made them."

The last of the ropes fall to his feet. "I'll explain later. Right now, I need you to trust me. Let's get these folks to safety." He squeezes my shoulder. "Is there another way out?" he asks Mr. Pipitone.

"This way."

We follow Mr. Pipitone to the darkest part of the basement. My legs cramp up from the ropes. They scream when I walk, but the muscles loosen with each step. Mr. Pipitone scrapes his hand against the wall, and suddenly we're drenched in light, facing a door. Could it be that easy? Open the door? Walk out?

Mr. Pipitone pushes open the door to . . . the laundry room.

Above the washer is a tiny window. The afternoon sun is low in the sky. How'd it get so late? A sliding glass pane cuts the window opening in half. None of us is getting through that window.

"If we take the glass out, I think Mick could fit." Mr. Pipitone gives me the once-over. "You're a skinny kid. You think you can crawl out through there?"

Before I can answer Mr. Pipitone, Mrs. Pipitone climbs on top of the washer with a screwdriver in her hand.

A deep voice bellows, "Hey! What're you do—"

Uncle George rams the Purnima brother standing

in the doorway, and they crash to the floor.

"Take him down!" Mr. Pipitone grabs the toolbox Mrs. Pipitone brought into the laundry room and drops it on top of the Purnima brother's head.

He rolls it off his head and sits up, the scratches on his face healing before our eyes.

"Get him in the laundry room!" Mrs. Pipitone yells.

It takes the five of us to shove him inside the laundry room and slam the door shut.

"Can we lock it?" I ask as we press our collective weight against the door.

Mrs. Pipitone stretches up and threads a tiny hook screwed into the top of the door through a tiny eye screwed into the doorframe. The whole thing pops off and shoots across the basement when the brother body slams the door.

"Oh my. Hold the door. I'll be right back."

When she returns, she's rolling a dusty treadmill. Brendan moves so she can jam it against the door. "I'll need help with other things."

"The dolly's under the stairs. Can you hold him while I get it?" Mr. Pipitone asks us.

"We got this," Uncle George says.

After what seems like hours and a lot of noise later, Mr. and Mrs. Pipitone have relocated a refrigerator, six cinder blocks, a box spring mattress, and a TV, and no one has to hold the door closed anymore.

Muffled snarls and banging creep from behind the basement belongings.

"That should keep him in one place for a little while." Mr. Pipitone adds the dolly to the pile.

"Until he finds the screwdriver I dropped and takes the door off the hinges."

"Or claws through the drywall with his bare hands," I offer.

Silence says it wasn't a good thing to mention.

"We should go. We need to find Neill and Cooper," Brendan finally says.

After we hurry up the stairs, Mr. Pipitone locks the basement door behind us. He shrugs his shoulders when he catches me shaking my head. "Maybe it will slow him down," he says.

"Sure," I tell him. Like poster board slows down a freight train. Adults. It's a wonder they survive as long as they do.

Locate the Others

PJ AND BOOGER-FACE ARE GONE. The weapons we stashed behind the bushes? Also gone. We circle around the house. Maybe they're hiding in the backyard.

"Brendan! Mick!" Neill runs from the lawnmower shed. "Am I glad to see you. Cooper's sleeping again. Should we get him a doctor? He doesn't look good. Keeps howling in his sleep."

When I look inside the shed, Cooper's snoring on top of a tarp. His legs and arms spasm like he's running on all fours.

"Those men stole our car keys and our cell phones." Mr. Pipitone looks over the fence into his neighbor's yard. "The Martins are away on vacation. We could try the Asners."

"They would've left for their family reunion by now," Mrs. Pipitone says.

Uncle George approaches them. "It's better not to involve your neighbors. They could get hurt. And I'm afraid a doctor won't know what to do with Cooper."

"Certainly we have to get in touch with his parents." Mr. Pipitone's lips tighten like he's sucking on a Sour Ball. I don't think he likes my uncle very much.

"The best thing for Cooper is to empty the shed of everything except him. Tie him up, lock him inside, and when he phases tonight, introduce some silver into his bloodstream."

I'm confused. "Why don't we just poke him with a silver fork right now?"

"The silver won't work until he's in wolf form. Mrs. Pipitone, do you have anything silver inside the house? Anything at all?"

"Um . . . well, I have some jewelry."

"We have that candelabra from my mother."

"No we don't. Not anymore. I sold it on eBay two years ago."

"But that was a wedding present!" Now it looks like the Sour Ball Mr. Pipitone is sucking on got stuck in his throat.

"The jewelry will work fine." Uncle George hands Mr. Pipitone the knife. "Cut him and then rub the–" He glances at Mrs. Pipitone.

"Necklace," she says.

"—necklace into the wound."

"Listen here." Mr. Pipitone hands back the knife. "I've seen some strange and horrible things in the last twenty-four hours, and I have a lunatic locked in my laundry room, but I am not about to tie up Brendan's friend and cut him with your knife. What I need to do is contact the police before the rest of the lunatics come back. Now I appreciate your help earlier, I truly do, but I think you should leave now."

Uncle George places his enormous hand on Mr. Pipitone's arm and talks low and slow, while Mr. Pipitone swallows that Sour Ball whole. "As soon as the moon is visible tonight, he won't be Brendan's friend. He'll be a monster in the shape of a wolf. A ravenous monster who won't know the difference between you and your family—or his family, or a doctor and his staff, or a station filled with police—from an all-you-can-eat buffet."

Mr. Pipitone considers my uncle's words better than if they'd come from me or Brendan. He looks at Cooper, who's traded running in his sleep for panting.

"I'll lock him in there, temporarily, but I won't tie him up. And . . . we'll have him wear the silver necklace. That should help, right? Without harming him?"

"Honestly? I don't know." He shakes his head. "I suppose it's worth a try. But you'll have to handle this on your own. Whether you involve police, parents, or doctors is up to you. This is where I leave you. I have a nephew to find."

❖ ❖ ❖

"Can't you sniff them out? Like a search-and-rescue dog?" Uncle George's truck is parked where we left it, the two scooters are still there, but Finley and Padraig are missing, and there's still no sign of Booger-Face and PJ.

"Only when I'm in wolf form is my nose of any use. I'm not like the Purnima brothers. They're enhanced with Padraig's blood. When I'm human, the only wolf traits I have are some extra strength and balance and a decent amount of wolf sense."

"Wolf sense?"

"Intuition."

I pop open the glove box. "Well, my Mick sense says maybe he left a note. That's what I would do."

"Yes. Maybe he did." Uncle George checks behind both sun visors. Nothing. Digs inside the center console. Nothing.

I peer behind the seats. More nothing. Jam my hands between the cushions. There's a melted Jolly Rancher, a gas receipt, but no note.

"Unless . . ."

"Unless what? Unless what?" This is my brother we're talking about. "What!"

"Unless they made it into the trailer."

"Wouldn't they come out when they heard us?"

"No. They don't know we're here." He pulls a notepad from the glove box. "There's a pen in the cup holder."

I retrieve it for him and he writes a message. Before I can read it, he tears off the page, hops down from the cab, and runs to the back of the truck. I have to scramble to catch up with him.

He runs his fingers along the side of the trailer door like he's looking for something. *Click, whir, slide.*

A plate-sized tray extends from the door. Uncle George places the note on the tray. *Whir, slide, click.* The tray disappears back into the trailer.

"They're in the trailer? Why can't we open it?" There's no handle, no latch. Pressing my hands on the door, there's no give either—the door's solid. I've never really paid attention to the trailer part of Uncle George's truck, even though I've ridden in the cab lots of times. He's never opened it for me, and I've never thought to ask.

In less than a minute, the trailer door rattles up and tucks out of sight. Finley, Padraig, Booger-Face, and PJ grin from inside the trailer like its Christmas Eve and Santa's staring at 'em through the doorway. Our jumble of homemade weapons waits in a pile.

"So that's how we get out!" Finley laughs.

"Pretty awesome truck you got here," Booger-Face says. "But what's with all the scratches? What kinda cargo you carry?"

Uncle George climbs into the trailer. I grab his hand so he can pull me in, and then watch him press numbers on a keypad on the wall.

The door rattles shut. Instead of pitching into darkness, the trailer roof blinks on a series of blue-lighted squares that make the inside of the trailer look like Smurf Village. The air is cool, not hot and stuffy like I expect. If I listen really hard, I hear the hum of a small motor.

PJ scoops a bunch of playing cards from the trailer bed and slips them into his fanny pack.

"That's what you've been doing all this time? Playing cards?" I rub my wrists, which are sore and red from where the ropes cinched me like a Thanksgiving turkey.

"Technically, we were hiding from circus werewolves," PJ says. "Padraig smelled them coming and came to warn us. He said we'd all be safe back here 'cause it's soundproof and smell proof."

"I thought I told you to stay in the cab."

"Um, technically, you said to stay in the truck," Finley says.

Padraig keeps looking at Uncle George like he wants to say something and he's waiting for the right time. Finally he says, "I'm the one who left the cab to get the others and bring them back here. Don't be mad at Finley. I haven't told them what I think this trailer's for. Maybe you should do that."

"Yes. Well." He rubs his fingers across some of the gouges in the trailer walls. Now that I'm paying attention, they're everywhere. Deep and shallow, long and short, splintered and smooth. Either he's transporting lions and tigers and bears back here, or . . .

I already know what Uncle George is gonna say when he sits and asks us to join him.

"This trailer is where I hide when I turn into a werewolf."

STEP 15

Hear the Story

UNCLE GEORGE MOSTLY looks at me and Finley when he talks. "I was twenty-five; you two weren't even born yet. That's almost fifteen years ago. I'd just finished community college. Got a job fixing computers in a big office building in downtown Atlanta. Good job. Wore a tie every day."

"Yuck." I wore a tie for four hours at the circus last night and can still feel it choking me.

"Ha! I hate 'em too now, Mick. Haven't worn one since . . . well, now I'm getting ahead of myself." Uncle George massages the back of his neck with his hand. "After working really late one night in November, I was backing out of my spot in the parking garage when I nearly ran over a guy. Knocked him to the ground.

"I jumped out of my car and rushed to where he landed. He was unconscious. No one else was around.

Couldn't get a good connection on my phone, so no 911. Did what I thought was right. I picked him up and put him in my back seat to drive him to the hospital myself."

He shakes his head. "My life would be a whole lot different if I'd left him there." Uncle George cracks his knuckles but stops when he catches us staring at him. "But I didn't leave him there. I put him in my car. While I drove, he woke up and started moaning. He was in some real pain. I thought I might've broken his ribs when I hit him, or made him worse when I carried him."

"Yes, you're supposed to leave accident victims where they are and let professionals move them, to prevent neck and spinal injuries." I give PJ the *not now* look. Honestly, the kid does not have to let us know *every* time his brain downloads a fact.

"Then he started growling. What I saw in my rear-view mirror scared me down to my core. I could barely breathe, but I managed to pull off the road.

"You see, it wasn't a guy in my back seat any more. It was a giant bear, or at least that was what I thought at first. Until he howled and ripped into me with his claws. Tore a hunk out of my shoulder. I scrambled out of the car, but the beast pounced on me. Believe it or not, I blocked his snapping jaws with my briefcase and then gave him a good wallop across the snout with it.

"But he recovered, and I had to use my forearm to keep him from my throat." Uncle George pivots his arm to show the scars.

Finley wrinkles his nose. "You said those were from a—"

"Dog attack," me and Uncle George say together.

"It sorta was." PJ examines the scars close up. "Dogs are descendants of wolves."

"Not *were*wolves." I'm not gonna argue further. I know my uncle lied to me and Finley when we asked him about his scars. He said a dog bit him when he was a kid. He did not say a man who changed into a wolf did it.

"Then what happened?" Padraig asks.

"He probably would've used me as his chew toy, but a couple driving by in a pickup slowed down to investigate. When they saw me and what I was fighting, they stopped to help. The driver took out a rifle and started shooting. He hit the wolf a couple times in the back. The wolf gave up on me and ran off into the fields. The guy with the rifle called an ambulance. The hospital stitched me up, and I was out in twenty-four hours." Uncle George checks his watch and then continues.

"They never found the 'animal' that attacked me. When I recovered my car at the tow yard, there were a bunch of shredded clothes in the back seat—"

Booger-Face interrupts, "What about his wallet?"

"No wallet. No ID. I went back to my apartment and tried to get back to my life. Only that didn't work out so well. First, it was dreams—or what I thought were dreams. Chasing rabbits. Always chasing rabbits. Then came the cravings: steaks, ribs, lamb chops. The rarer the better. I couldn't keep a shave through the day. Had to trim my nails every morning and my nose hairs every night. I got short-tempered from lack of sleep and lost my job. Started working odd jobs here and there. Moved around from state to state.

"It all went south when I woke up one morning naked in the woods, miles away from my apartment."

"That's when you knew?" Finley asks, his eyes as big as dinner plates in his kid-sized head.

"No. More like, I didn't want to know. Which was my mistake. Every thirty days or so, for two to three days at a time, I would find myself in some strange place, usually buck naked, usually with blood on me—not my own—and sometimes with an animal carcass near me: a dear, a coyote, a wild pig, one time a mountain lion." Uncle George looks at his watch again. I want to say something about him checking the time, but

I don't want to barge in.

"It wasn't until I bit Frido Purnima that I realized what I really was and what I had to do." He picks at his nails, and I notice they're longer since this morning. His five-o'clock shadow has morphed into a half-inch scruff. Why did I never notice this stuff the other times Uncle George came visiting? I can't believe how clueless I've been.

"I was one of the cooks at a diner in Chattanooga when the brothers came in. They were rowdy. Ordered a bunch of nonstandard stuff. Harassed the waitstaff. Trust me, these guys were jerks long before they became werewolves. I brought out their food personally, and Frido threw it in my face. Covered me in the meal I'd just made. I threw them out of the diner and the night manager fired me. 'The customer is always right,' he said."

"My mom grits her teeth whenever she says that." Booger-Face demonstrates and Uncle George laughs.

"Well, I did worse. Much worse. I followed them out to the parking lot. Apparently, I phased in front of them all, took a chunk out of Frido's leg, and then ran away."

"He turned the next night," Padraig says. "His brothers tried to control him, but he bit them all. Or at least that's how they tell it."

"They seemed a close bunch. Doesn't surprise me."

Uncle George stares at me then, and his eyes are wet. "The thing is, biting Frido? I remember doing it. That's when I bought the truck and made sure I stayed away from your mom and you boys. I had to time my visits right 'cause I couldn't risk hurting you."

And all this time I thought it was Uncle George's job that made his visits scarce.

"Some college buddies helped me trick out the trailer. The blue lights help."

"'Cause they're calming?" PJ asks. "The color blue helps people feel focused and serene."

"That's right. Plus the trailer can only be locked and unlocked on the inside by a code entered with human fingerprints."

"So you lock yourself in on the night of a full moon while you're still human, and let yourself out when you're not a wolf anymore." Finley clicks his tongue against his teeth as he puts the puzzle together.

"Yes. Then I can keep everyone safe."

"Then how'd Finley and the rest get back here?" I scan the keypad strapped to the wall.

"I must've left the inside and outside locks unlocked."

"We got back here no problem," Finley says. "But PJ fell against the keypad and locked us in. We didn't know how to get out until that drawer opened with your note inside."

"We still have our cell phones, but they don't work in here. Good thing you figured out where we were." Booger-Face stands and helps the rest of us up. "I always thought your uncle was cool. Now I know he's the coolest ever."

PJ chimes in. "I wish I had an uncle who was a werewolf."

What, are my friends crazy? "No! He doesn't have to be a werewolf anymore. We know how to fix him. Tonight, when he changes, we'll stab him with silver and he'll be normal again." I grab my uncle's arm and imagine I feel the hair growing beneath my fingers. "Then you can help us change back all the Purnima brothers. And Cooper, too."

He stares at me long and hard with watery, blood-shot eyes. "Sorry, Mick, but I'll be locking myself up tonight as usual. You'll have to change the Purnima brothers yourself, with the help of your friends here. I want to stay a werewolf."

STEP 16

Leave Someone Behind

"WHY? WE CAN CURE YOU!" My uncle must've been a werewolf too long. It's affected his brain.

Finley stands beside me. "We need your help, Uncle George."

Booger-Face places his palm against five deep grooves in the trailer wall. "We can't take on seven werewolves without you."

"Eight, if we count Cooper," PJ adds.

"Eight werewolves." I'm glad someone was keeping track. "And there's only five of us. Neill's with Cooper, Brendan's with his parents, and you talked to them—they're not going to help." Why would my uncle *choose* to be a wolf-man?

Uncle George holds up his hand until we calm down. "I know it sounds crazy, but I need to be a werewolf a little longer. I've been tracking down the guy who turned me. I need to find out if he's the alpha, and if he is, I can stop all of this for good. That's why I couldn't take you to the circus last night–I was following a lead. Normally I wouldn't be anywhere near Beachwood during a full moon. Since I wasn't gonna be able to visit last night, you weren't going to see me until Tuesday."

"Did you think one of the Purnima brothers was your guy?"

"Yes. When Mick told me the situation, I thought one of your circus werewolves must be the alpha. Until I recognized Frido and realized my mistake." He shakes his head. "Frido is my creation, and by rights I should be the one to undo what I've done, but I can't risk losing my wolf sense and the alpha's trail along with it. He's still out there. I have to find him.

"I have faith in you." He squeezes my shoulder. "You've got great Mick sense, and you're a good leader." He covers his mouth with his other hand and coughs sharply. "You can do this." His last words come out all gravelly, like something's caught in his throat.

The hand on my shoulder trembles. The fingers stretch on top of my shirt, skin blackening, hair lengthening. A groan, deep and guttural, squeezes from between Uncle George's teeth. Teeth that get bigger and sharper before my eyes.

"Uncle George?" Finley whimpers.

"Leave." He growls. "Now."

"He won't be able to enter the code. He doesn't have human fingers anymore!" PJ screams to be heard over my uncle's grunts and moans.

"Finley's got the note with the code." PJ tries to put as much space between himself and Uncle George as he can. I swear, if he could shimmy up the wall like Spiderman, he would.

Uncle George is barely recognizable, covered in black hair, crouched on the trailer bed.

I position myself between him and Finley like a goalie protecting the net. "Go ahead. Enter the code."

Finley struggles to unfold the note. His hands shake as he starts to press the keys.

"Wait! We can't let your uncle escape. When you open the door, he could make a run for it before you close it again." Booger-Face backs away from the wolf-man trapped with us in the trailer.

Saliva drips from Uncle George's gaping maw of sharp teeth. He shudders, and every bit of human vibrates from his face.

Grrrrrr.

This growl comes from behind me. I take my eyes off Uncle George for a second to look. Padraig's morphed into his wolf-boy self. He's half the size of Uncle George but just as fierce looking. His teeth flash, his red hair stands on end along his spine.

The keypad beeps and the door rolls upward.

Padraig crouches on his haunches, blocking the exit. His lips curl back in a snarl as my uncle the werewolf glares and snarls back at him.

"The weapons! Go! Go!" Booger-Face scoops the bundle of spears and the container of arrows into his arms. A handful of the spears slips from his grasp and scatters across the truck bed. While the werewolves dance around each other, roaring and snapping, I grab one of the spears. Booger-Face throws the weapons he has left to the grass and jumps out of the truck, right before my uncle skids into him.

Circling to face my uncle werewolf, Padraig nips at his face and feet to get him to slowly back away from the opening door.

PJ grabs the bow in one hand and the boomerang in the other. He stumble-trips to the edge of the trailer, and Booger-Face pulls him out.

A spear in my hand, I approach the two werewolves. I could stab Uncle George in the back right now. Launch the spines of PJ's silver fork into his bloodstream right now. Cure him forever. Right now.

Breaths deep and steady, I raise the spear and tense my arm muscles, readying my wrist, aiming the forked end between my uncle's furry shoulder blades. Silently,

I count to three.

One. Two. Two and half.

The door is halfway open. Finley presses the code into the keypad again. He stares at the door, reversing on its track.

Why isn't he leaving the truck? Why isn't he moving?

Move . . . move . . . MOVE.

OK, then, I'll move you.

I toss down the spear and pounce on my brother, encircling him like a boa constrictor. Then I dive, tuck, roll.

My uncle the werewolf leaps toward the closing door, jaws snapping, spit spraying, his hot breath coating my back and neck. Padraig barrels into him and sends him sprawling backward.

Me and Finley drop to the ground. "Padraig!" I shout. He's going to get trapped inside with Uncle George. "No!"

The smaller werewolf flattens himself and squeezes through the narrow opening. The door clamps shut on the tip of his tail and he yelps. A handful of red fur sticks out from the trailer, but Padraig is safe outside. With the door closed, not even werewolf noises escape. My uncle was right: it is soundproof.

"You OK?"

Padraig rubs his head against my hand.

"You understand me?"

He tilts his head, flicks his ears, and blinks once.

Yes! Even a Canadian werewolf knows the blinking code.

"Look, Mick. Moon's up," Booger-Face says.

While we were hiding out in the trailer, distracted by my uncle's story, the afternoon came and went. Evening found its way to Beachwood, and the moon's glowing in the sky before the sun's even set.

Padraig spots the moon too and lifts his snout. He inhales deeply.

"Uh-oh." I know what's coming, and I wince as I brace myself.

Ow-wooooooo. Ow-ow-owoooooo. Ow-ow-owoooooooo.

"Shh, shh." PJ covers his ears.

"No. It's OK, PJ. Howl all you want, Padraig." Finley grins. "I think I know what to do."

Round Up the Pack

EVERY DOG IN THE NEIGHBORHOOD picks up Padraig's call. It almost sounds like the cats and birds are getting involved too. The racket bounces off fences and echoes from open windows.

The gears behind Finley's eyes spark and turn.

"What is it? Whatcha got, little bro?"

"The dogs. Padraig's talking to them. They can help us."

Padraig stops howling to blink his eyes at me. He also wags his tail, which is a good sign he's psyched for Finley's idea.

"OK. Go on."

"The dogs can keep their people inside and busy so they're outta the way and safe. The strays—they can help us with the Purnima brothers."

"Then we can poke 'em." Booger-Face thrusts a spear

in the air.

"I have more."

I nod. Finley's on a roll.

"The Purnima brothers want Padraig. We should put Padraig where we want them to go. Somewhere with a good view and places we can hide. Somewhere we know really well that's away from people: the dump."

It's a solid plan. A great plan. "Let's do it."

Finley beams.

"We've only got six spears. The rest are stuck inside the trailer. I need to bind them together again so I can carry them." Booger-Face uses an arrow tip to rip a hole in the bottom of his T-shirt. He tears off the bottom half. Now he's wearing a crop top.

My eyes scan his balloon-shaped belly. "You're brave."

He pulls something fuzzy from his belly button. "It's not the first shirt I've ruined. Won't be the last, either." He ties up the spears with the shirt scrap. "Hey, maybe I can ride on Padraig's back."

Padraig curls his lips. *Grrrrrrrrr.*

"OK, OK. You're not big enough anyway." He straddles PJ's scooter, propping the spear bundle across the handlebars with one hand and plopping a helmet onto his head with the other. "Let's ride."

PJ jumps on the seat in front of him and fires up

the engine.

"Sorry, buddy. One helmet left. You're younger."
I hand the unicorn helmet to Finley.

He rolls his eyes and straps the sparkly helmet on.

Booger-Face and PJ on one scooter with the spears, and me and Finley on the other with the bow, the quiver, and the boomerang, take off toward the dump. Padraig lopes alongside, stopping now and then to howl.

Before long, there's at least a dozen dogs running with us and . . . is that Bagel Boy? I grin, feeling better already. Bagel Boy is a great addition to our team.

If anyone looks out their window, we'll wind up on YouTube for sure. But all the houses we pass are either dark or all lit up while a nutzoid barking-screeching-shouting turmoil occupies the people inside.

"It's working," Finley yells over the whine of the scooter's motor. "Only a little ways now."

The snarl is so loud it sends a stampede of heebie-jeebies racing down my spine. To my left, a pair of red eyes blazing from a hairy face keep pace with mine. The second snarl is on my right, attached to another pair of glowing red eyes.

One of the dogs running with us nips at the wolf on the left. The wolf snatches the dog by the nape and tosses it aside like an empty bag of chips. Another werewolf flanks us. Then another. And another. They bump against the dogs, squeezing us into a smaller space.

"They're moving us!" Finley shouts.

He's right. They're herding us. Away from the dump and toward the fairgrounds. Toward the circus.

We can't let them take us to the circus. I rev the scooter's engine and burst in front of PJ. Hopefully he understands the hand signal for stop in the fading light. I weave in front of him so he'll slow down.

He spins out, nearly throwing himself and Booger-Face over the handlebars. I stop next to him and reach out to steady his scooter so he doesn't fall over.

Padraig paces in the center of our pack of dogs. They have their backs to him, facing the five werewolves that encircle us.

Booger-Face slides a spear out of the bundle and hops off PJ's scooter. I grab the bow and quickly nock an arrow.

One of the werewolves, a big ugly beast with extralong ears, approaches fast, head down, lips curled back in a snarl, saber teeth glistening in the streetlight.

Finley swings his leg off the scooter in one swift movement and whips his boomerang at the advancing werewolf. The boomerang picks up speed in the air and clobbers the wolf across the muzzle. He yelps.

Instantly, everyone and everything moves. Dogs leap. Werewolves pounce. Booger-Face gets a good stab to the back leg of the long-eared werewolf.

He yipes like a Chihuahua and dashes behind a nearby bush, but not before I see his hairy wolf leg morph into a hairy man leg.

"You got one!"

Now the other werewolves are wary. They stay just out of reach of Booger-Face and his spear. I fire my arrow at a black werewolf with a broad face and a flat snout, intending to hit him in the leg. My arrow skids across the asphalt, and the werewolf steps on the shaft, breaking it in two.

Booger-Face pokes him in the rump while he's distracted. Werewolf two yelps and scampers off.

The three remaining werewolves circle Booger-Face and separate him from the rest of us. He thrusts his spear at one, who effectively dodges. This is bad. Really bad. If they rush him, he's a goner.

The bow is heavy in my hands. I'm no Avenger. I skid over to PJ and push the bow into his arms. I sling the quiver over his shoulders. "Help him."

Finley joins us. "Together." He arcs his boomerang while PJ releases an arrow.

The boomerang slams into a tan werewolf's face, sending him sprawling. PJ's arrow lands in that same werewolf's withers. Dogs pounce, yapping and snarling. A breath later, another arrow lands in a gray werewolf's leg.

Booger-Face tumbles to the ground in the frenzy. His spear clatters out of reach. The last werewolf lunges at Booger-Face, jaws spread, teeth bared. Booger-Face throws out his arm to protect his neck.

The werewolf never reaches him. An arrow sticks from his haunches.

"Ow. Ow. Ow," the man squeals before running off.

"PJ, you're amazing." I clap him on the back. "You too, Finley. What an arm." I retrieve Booger-Face's spear and help him off the ground. "Awesome job."

He takes the spear and grins. "That last one got close."

Padraig prances over, wagging his tail.

Before he reaches us, a huge brown werewolf leaps from the shadows and snatches Padraig by the nape. He carries him off, followed by a second, smaller werewolf. They sprint down the road.

Don't Lose Your Nerve

"THEY'RE GETTING AWAY!"

We scramble back onto the scooters. The dogs chase after Padraig ahead of us, and we follow the dogs. The scooters squeal as we push them to their limits. We're not fast enough. The barks fade away with the last of the sunlight.

PJ stops and I pull up next to him. "There were two of them. They waited until we weren't paying attention."

"I forgot how many brothers there were. I thought we got them all." Finley pounds his fist into his hand.

"You know they'll bite the other brothers and make them werewolves again." Booger-Faces's shoulders slump. "I should go home. My parents are gonna worry about me being gone all day."

"We can't give up," I tell them. "Come on. We know they're going back to the circus. Those dogs aren't giving up. They'll help."

"And the brothers will have help too. Auguste Linville, Shrunken-Head Man, everyone who works there has to know what the Purnima brothers are. They'll protect them. We can't fight all those people. I should call Nanny. She's gonna wonder about me too."

"Call on your cells and tell them you're with me. Look, we broke Padraig out once. We'll just have to do it again. Me and Finley . . . we need you guys."

Booger-Face sighs. "OK. I guess we gotta try. Padraig doesn't deserve to be locked up again."

"How 'bout you?"

PJ bows his head. "Padraig's my friend now." He turns his headlight on. "Yes. I'm in." He tears off and I follow his taillight.

❖ ❖ ❖

The circus isn't as crowded tonight. In fact, it's nearly empty. Either everyone in town went last night, or word got out to avoid it this year. We park the scooters next to a bike rack and head for the entrance with our weapons.

"Wait. Me and Finley don't have money for tickets, and we can't bring these through the front gate." I shake a spear in the air.

"We can if we're dressed like performers." Booger-Face points to the trailers. "One of those has got to be a dressing room." He runs toward them before any of us have a chance to argue.

Darting behind parking signs and porta-potties, I crouch-run and avoid being seen by a woman in a leotard while she bends to stretch. Finley zigzags over next, and then PJ, who manages to trip twice before he joins us.

I don't get it. "How can you be such a good shot, but you run like a . . . a . . ."

"Dodo bird? My mom says I'm extra clutzy 'cause I'm going to have a growth spurt."

I hide a snicker behind my hand. "If that's true, your growth spurt's gonna be amazing. You could work here as the world's tallest man."

"This is the one." Finley points to a trailer with COSTUMES stenciled on its side. He cracks open the door and then slips inside, and I wonder when he got so brave. Last night he was hanging on to me like a baby koala.

He peeks out the door and waves us in using Cooper's Native American sign language, and now I'm thinking about Cooper and how the shed's working out for him. Hope he hasn't eaten anyone.

Booger-Face elbows me. "Come on."

Inside the trailer, a forest of costumes hangs on racks in rows. Dressing tables with lighted mirrors line the wall. I set the weapons down and scan the rainbow of clothing in front of me.

"We don't have time to shop." Booger-Face tosses me a green suit and a yellow felt hat. PJ's already wearing a stretchy blue outfit with a sequined cape that's so sparkly it stabs my eyes.

The clothes are big enough I can slide them over top the one's I'm wearing. I catch a glimpse of myself in one of the mirrors. I'm a giant leprechaun.

"Here." Booger-Face hands me a green squishy ball. "It's a nose. People will think we're clowns."

That's when I notice his outfit. "Are those tights?"

He punches me in the arm.

"Ow. What's that for?"

"Just 'cause."

"We should go," Finley says. He's wearing a polka-dotted jumper and a red frizzy wig. Smeary clown makeup decorates his face.

"You're scary looking, kiddo."

"Good." He grabs his boomerang. "I'll fit right in."

❖ ❖ ❖

We walk right through the employees-only side entrance. Apparently clowns with weapons are as normal as roasted peanuts at the A. Linville & Purnima Bros. Circus.

"Where to first? Madam Mayhem's?" Booger-Face looks like a cross between a ballerina and a pirate.

"They wouldn't put him in the same cage he escaped from." Something cold and wet rests in my palm. "Bagel Boy!"

He noses me again and then bounds away.

"Follow him."

We chase after the dog, who leads us to the back of the Purnima brothers' performance tent. CLOSED UNTIL FURTHER NOTICE. NO ENTRY PERMITTED hangs above the tent flaps, which are strapped down and fastened with a small padlock.

I pull out one of the arrows from my quiver and use the arrowhead to saw through the straps that pin the flaps closed at the bottom. PJ's dad's grinder made the tips of the arrows nice and sharp, so it doesn't take too long to cut through the material.

Bagel Boy noses underneath the flaps, and we crawl in after him.

Chained to a stake in the center of the ring, Padraig's in wolf form still. Bagel Boy lopes over, slurps his face, and then lies next to him, head on his paws.

"Let's hide here." I point to the stands.

It's dark and cool underneath the risers, and we have a good view of most of the tent. Too bad it smells like molding food, animal dung, and sweat.

Booger-Face ditches his pirate hat near a stack of empty popcorn boxes. "We should get him. There's no one here."

"How're we gonna free him without a key?" Finley asks.

"We can dig up the stake and get him out of the cuff later. Man, it's gross under here." Booger-Face transfers something pink and sticky from his hand to his tights. Might be bubble gum. Might be strawberry syrup. Might be cotton-candy barf.

"What're we gonna dig with?" Finley asks.

"The spears?"

"They're made from forks. Digging into the ground is not like digging into mashed potatoes." My stomach growls. I haven't eaten in almost twenty-four hours. Now all I can think about is using a spear to dig into a truckload of garlic mashed potatoes mixed with cream cheese and an acre of melted butter. Naw, forget the spear. I'll just dive in headfirst.

"Did you hear me? Mick?"

"What?"

"Why can't Padraig dig his own stake out?" Finley

asks, and suddenly his head looks like a baked potato. I shake the image away.

"Yeah. We'll tell him 'dig,' and he can tell Bagel Boy. They've got the paws to do it." Now Booger-Face's face has morphed into a giant tater tot.

"OK. Let's go out there and protect them while they dig." PJ ties a double knot in his cape and takes off running.

I hesitate. There's a gnawing in my gut that isn't potato cravings. Why hasn't Padraig thought to dig himself free on his own?

Booger-Face rushes after PJ before I can tell him my worries.

Finley wrinkles his nose. "What's wrong?"

"Something's not right. It seems too easy. Like . . . like . . ."

"A trap."

"Exactly."

When Booger-Face and PJ skid to a stop in the center of the ring, Padraig head-butts Booger-Face and Bagel Boy nips at PJ's heels, which is so not like Bagel Boy. Usually that dog slobbers on my friends, he doesn't snap at them.

I hold Finley back. "They don't want us out there."

A blinding spot of light breaks through the dark tent and lands on the center ring. One after the other, sections of tent lights flash on.

From behind a large wagon, Auguste Linville and Shrunken-Head Man appear, followed by Top Hat Guy and some other guy I don't recognize. They carry torches and grim expressions. Shrunken-Head Man raises something long and black from behind his back.

Air squeaks from my lungs. My friends are sitting ducks. I consider waving my arms and yelling, "Over here!"

Shrunken-Head Man, what is his name? The Three-Eyed Lady told me. Her name was Carlotta and he was . . . Rocky!

Rocky hands a megaphone to Auguste, who brings the mouthpiece to his face. "Just in time, boys. We need some more clowns in our circus. We seem to be short a few."

The two werewolves that snatched Padraig in the street enter from behind the four men. Top Hat Guy waves his torch at one that comes too close.

That's why they have torches. To protect themselves from the werewolves.

The werewolves trot into the ring. Bagel Boy's hair stands on end; he looks like a golden lint ball. Padraig growls. Booger-Face points a spear and backs up next to PJ. PJ whips his head around like he's searching for something.

"He forgot the bow," Finley whispers and points a couple feet ahead of us.

The bow and quiver of arrows lies against the lowest riser.

Padraig howls and soon Bagel Boy joins in. Barking in the distance gets louder as it gets closer.

"They're calling reinforcements."

Finley grabs his boomerang. "Now?"

"Wait for the dogs."

Padraig stops howling to dig at his stake.

One of the werewolves sneaks toward him.

A dozen or more dogs stream through the opening we made in the tent. Dogs with collars and tags. Filthy strays. Circus dogs in costume. Purebreds. Mutts. A puppy.

"Now!"

Finley whips his boomerang through the air and clocks a werewolf in the back of the head. The werewolf wobbles a second, shakes his head, and then he spots us. His eyes glow brighter and he charges toward us, snarling.

"Shoot him, Mick. Shoot him!"

I fire an arrow and miss him by a mile. "I can't do it. Run."

A handful of dogs intercepts the werewolf, but he tosses them aside like chew toys.

"We can't outrun him. You have to shoot him." Finley hands me another arrow as the werewolf closes in.

What did PJ tell me? Breathe in when I draw back. Keep my elbow up. Release my breath and my arrow at the same time. The tip of my arrow nicks the werewolf's ear.

We're going to die.

Me and Finley scramble below the risers. Finley pulls his leg in at the same time the werewolf's jaws snap closed, spit spraying from his—human lips. Hair fades from his face. His eyes are the last to change, from red to blue.

"Ha! His ear's bleeding. You got him, Mick. You got him."

The man yanks his arm away from us and twists his hand in front of his face. "I'm me," he says under his breath. "I can go home."

He's Frido. Only a smaller version, not all pumped up on Padraig's blood. There's only one werewolf left. Hopefully Booger-Face has been able to hold him off with his spear.

"Come on!" Me and Finley crawl out from under the risers.

The dogs form a semicircle around Booger-Face, PJ, and Padraig, shielding them from the werewolf.

Sort of. He's advancing through them, tossing them from his path, but they scuttle to their feet and rejoin the barricade.

Until Top Hat Guy runs at the dogs with his torch. Several run away yelping. The other three men join in, waving their torches at the dogs, who scatter.

Auguste left his megaphone. It gleams in the tent lights like a beacon, and I sprint for it. Heavier than I expect, it takes me a second to steady it in front of my face. Fingers and toes crossed this works.

"MUCOUS." My one word booms through the tent.

Realization slides across Booger-Face's face. Without hesitating, he inhales deeply and then launches a roaring snot rocket of epic awesomeness. The booger bomb arcs over the dogs like a comet with a stretchy slime tail and lands on the four men with a resounding *splat*. Their torch flames sizzle out, and the men sink to their knees under the weight of snot.

"What is this?"

"It's in my eyes."

"I can't breathe."

The men bat helplessly at the boogers coating them like they've been dipped in clear molasses.

"Mick. Over there. It's Frido," Finley says.

Wearing only a circus flag for a skirt, Frido runs toward PJ and Booger-Face, carrying a spear in the air like a javelin. "Aargh!" he screams as he runs.

"Stop him. Stop him!" Finley yells. "He's going for PJ."

Booger-Face points his spear in Frido's direction. But Frido's *not* going for PJ. He's not even looking at PJ.

"No. It's OK." I hold Finley back and shout into the megaphone. "Booger-Face, get out of the way."

The werewolf leaps toward Booger-Face, who's turned toward Frido and doesn't see him. Frido hurls the spear.

"Duck," I yell through the megaphone.

Booger-Face flattens, and the spear sticks right between the werewolf's eyes. The werewolf lurches backward. Dust puffs around his fur when he lands.

Frido drops next to him and yanks out the spear. He hugs his brother. "It's over."

Me and Finley rush over to the guys. Bagel Boy licks my hand and then he barks twice. The other dogs gallop from the tent. He wags his tail and almost seems to smile at us before he dashes after the dogs.

Booger-Face dusts himself off. Now he's more filthy kid than pirate or ballerina.

PJ drapes his sparkly cape over Padraig. "You can change back now."

Padraig ducks underneath the cape, which wiggles

for a moment, and then the boy peers out. "Thank you."

"What about them?" Finley points at the four slimed men. Frido and his brother have already disappeared.

Grrrrrrrrrrr.

"Oh no. No. No." I recognize a werewolf growl anywhere.

In the direction of the sound, two more werewolves enter the ring.

"There were seven brothers. Not nine. Seven." Finley kicks at the ground.

"There's more? I thought we got them all?" PJ picks up Booger-Face's spear. "Did a couple get rebit?"

I block Finley. "Stand behind me."

Their red eyes gleam. Their ears twitch. Their muscles roll beneath thick fur. Slowly, the two werewolves move toward us.

STEP 19

Lead the Team

"MOM! DAD!"

The werewolves pounce on Padraig and rub against him playfully. The larger one turns toward the slime-coated men and bares his teeth.

I didn't know grown men could squeal like little girls. But they can. And they do. Right before they run to the exit with a werewolf chomping at their back-sides.

"Yay, Dad," Padraig laughs.

The other werewolf, who must be Padraig's mom, disappears out the back and returns with a bundle in her mouth. She drops it near Padraig.

"Thanks, Mom." He unties the top and fabric spills out. He starts laying out three sets of clothes. "Privacy, guys."

The four of us make ourselves scarce by retrieving

our weapons. I grab the megaphone, too.

"Whatcha want with that?" Finley asks.

"Circus souvenir."

"I don't want a souvenir. I don't ever want to go to the circus again."

PJ joins us. "Me either."

"Give it some time. You might change your minds," a soft voice says. It's Padraig's mom. Padraig's parents are people now, fully clothed with hands to shake.

"Mom and Dad, these are my friends."

"Thank you for saving my boy." Padraig's dad pumps my hand. "If you ever need anything. Any of you." He grabs Finley's hand, then PJ's, and finally Booger-Face's.

"And you're welcome to visit anytime. Anytime," Padraig's mom says.

My brain's not sure how to ask the question, so my mouth does the hard work for me. "We need a ride. It's really too far to walk, and our scooters don't have enough gas. Do you mind turning back into werewolves and carrying us on your backs?"

Padraig's mom raises her eyebrows. "I don't think that will be necessary."

"We drove." Padraig's dad laughs when he looks at me. "As people. We drove the rental car here as people."

"Come on dorkhead, where do you want us to take you?" Padraig grins.

I focus on the goal and not on what a dufus I am. "We need to go back to the Pipitones'."

No one notices when we make our exit, mostly because everyone's paying attention to the four men surrounded by police officers by the front entrance. Through a gap in the crowd, I see Top Hat Guy's finally lost his top hat. It's crushed on the ground beside his feet. Auguste Linville has his hands cuffed behind his back. Frido and one of his brothers are off to the side, chatting with a guy who's taking notes.

Not sure what's going down. Maybe the brothers turned in their circus bosses. Looks like the end of the A. Linville & Purnima Bros. Circus. Instead of feeling sad, I'm just glad someone other than me's getting in trouble.

Padraig's mom and dad each take one of his hands as we follow them to their car. Yeah, someone oughta go to jail for kidnapping a kid and keeping him from his parents.

❖ ❖ ❖

The full moon shines high and bright in a clear sky when we arrive at the Pipitones'. Voices and music carry on the breeze from their backyard. A small fire glows, surrounded by shadows in lawn chairs. The door to the shed is wide open. There aren't any howls or snarls. No claws shredding wood. Did Mr. Pipitone change his mind about putting silver into Cooper's blood?

When I get closer, Neill rises to greet me. "Mick, look what Cooper can do." He snags a hot dog from a plate. "Come, Cooper. Come here, boy."

A small, yellow-haired werewolf bounds out of the darkness.

"Sit. Siiiiiiiit. Good." Neill tosses him the hot dog, and the werewolf snatches it out of the air and gulps it down.

"You've got to be kidding me." It's hard to believe what I'm seeing.

"It's the silver necklace. I put it on him before he turned." Brendan ruffles Cooper's fur. "When the guy in the laundry room turned, he went ballistic. Tore through the barrier. Tore both the basement and the front doors down. Did you see him?"

"Oh yeah, we saw him." Booger-Face holds his spear. He's probably going to sleep with it.

"But Cooper didn't go crazy. He's just a big dog." Neill scratches behind one of Cooper's pointy ears.

PJ says aloud what I'm thinking inside. "If I'm ever a werewolf, please don't teach me to sit and pat me on the head."

"Hope he doesn't remember," Finley says.

Padraig and his parents are talking to Mr. and Mrs. Pipitone, so they don't see me pull an arrow from my quiver.

"What're you doing? You're not gonna shoot him, are you?" Brendan holds up his hands.

"No. I'm not a very good shot." I jab the arrowhead into Cooper's nape using only my hand, and he yelps.

Finley grabs a blanket from one of the lawn chairs and throws it over Cooper as his paws change into hands.

Cooper pokes his head out and burps. "How come I taste hot dogs? I hate hot dogs. Marissa said that her cousin knows a butcher who told her hot dogs are made from the pig parts he throws away."

"Welcome back, Cooper," Booger-Face says.

"Where'd I go? Hey, did you know one of those guys from the circus bit me?" He extends his arm out from the blanket. "Hey, the bite's gone." He wraps the blanket closer. "Why am I naked under here?"

I lead him to a chair by the fire. "I have something to tell you, and you're gonna need to sit for it."

Booger-Face snickers. "Yeah. Sit, Cooper. Sit."

Face a Fear

"THAT'S SOME STORY, Mick. Wish I'd had the chance to say good-bye to Padraig and meet his parents." Uncle George swallows the last of his grilled cheese sandwich and chases it with a swig of Coke.

Me and Finley already finished ours. I dig out another handful of chips and plop them on my plate.

"Not as good as your Mom's cooking, I know." He runs his hand through his wet hair.

Something else I didn't notice before: my uncle takes a lot of showers. Now I know he's been trying to wash away his dog smell.

"Food's fine." Mom's at work, so grilled cheese and chips for breakfast is about as good as it gets.

"Sounds like you did better than fine taking on those werewolves. Saving Padraig from the circus. You're a great leader."

"I didn't lead. I was mostly just there. Finley was taking out werewolves with his boomerang. Booger-Face dropped a couple with his spear. Plus he stopped four grown men in their tracks with his super snot. And PJ—jeez, PJ's a real-live Hawkeye. Even Brendan and his monkey toes is the one who got us out of the basement."

Finley's plate clatters in the sink. "None of that would've happened without you."

"Look at me, Mick," Uncle George says. "Finley told me how hard it was for you to honor my wishes and not change me back to human in the truck. That took real courage."

"I almost went through with it."

"But you didn't. Sometimes being a leader is about taking a step back and not taking action. Letting others lead. Playing to their strengths. Going with your gut."

"Mick sense," I say.

"Yes. You said it yourself to me in the truck. You've got good instincts, Mick. That's why your friends rely on you."

"Yeah." I think back to all the times my friends looked to me for answers. Even if I didn't have the answers, I could tell when someone else did.

"You saved Cooper from being Neill and Brendan's pet," Finley adds. "Cooper's going to be loyal forever.

Oh. Wait." He frowns and shakes his head. "That makes him sound like he's still a dog."

"Ha. I did, didn't I? About that . . ." I root through my shorts pocket, pull out a small box, and slide it across the table to Uncle George. "I got something for you. Well, it's not just from me. It's from all of us: me and Finley, PJ, Booger-Face, Neill and Cooper, and the Pipitones, too. We all chipped in."

"What's this?"

"Open it."

Uncle George lifts the lid. "Well look at that. It's nice, but if it's real silver, I can't touch it."

"It's silver, all right, and you can touch it. Cooper proved it. Put it on. It'll make your time as a werewolf easier. Like Cooper's."

"So I'll be more like a dog than a wolf?"

"If you want. You get to decide. Wear it when you want to be safe around people. Like mom and me and Finley. Don't wear it when you want to go full-blown wolf-man, like when you finally find the alpha. Now you have a choice."

Uncle George prods the silver with his index finger. When nothing happens, he scoops up the necklace. A silver wolf pendant flashes from a silver chain. He slips it over his head and tucks it inside his shirt. "Nice. Feels . . . calming. Thanks, guys. Tell everyone thanks."

His smile slides off his face and he gets all serious again. "You OK with all this? Keeping my secret from your mom?"

"She might be more understanding than you think." She's mom to me, after all. She puts up with a lot of weird. "Look at PJ's driver, Gene. He doesn't even blink when we tell him about monster stuff. And Nanny. PJ told her the truth right away."

"Yeah, and now we gotta help him polish everything shiny in his house." Finley crosses his arms.

"She still mad about the missing silverware?"

"Let's just say there's an awful lot of shiny stuff at PJ's," I tell him.

"And Nanny's gonna supervise us. It's gonna be a very . . . long . . . day."

Uncle George chuckles. "It'll go faster with all of you helping." He fingers the wolf on his necklace and stares off at something I can't see. "Let me think about telling your mom. She's a pretty strong woman. Maybe . . . maybe she can handle knowing her brother's a werewolf."

"Sure she can," I reassure him. "Be brave and just talk to her." He's gotta know life's gonna be better when his family has his back.

Riiiiiiiiiiiiing.

"I got it." Finley snatches the receiver from the wall. "Hi . . . Yeah . . . Cool . . . I'll get him." He holds the phone out to me. "Savannah's calling from China. She says it's like 1:00 in the morning there."

"Why's she calling?"

"She says she has to ask you something before she loses her nerve." He waves the phone at me. "Come on, bro. Be brave. You battled werewolves, you can talk to Savannah." His grin gets my Mick sense buzzing.

The phone weighs a thousand pounds. I clear my throat twice, but my voice still comes out like I swallowed rocks instead of chips. "Hey, Savannah."

"Hey, Mick. It's late here, and I promised my parents I'd be quick. You know that dance at school the Friday after we get back from spring break? Will you go with me? . . . Mick? . . . You still there?"

Mick and the Team's List of Materials for How to Protect Your Neighborhood from Circus Werewolves
OR, WHAT WE LEARNED TO HAVE WITH US
NEXT TIME

1. Silver forks, for stabbing werewolves. Obvious!
2. A silver chain, with or without pendant, for calming werewolves. Who knew?
3. Motorized scooters, for zipping around town and herding werewolves.
4. Friends. Trust us on this; you can't protect your neighborhood from circus werewolves all by yourself.
5. A candy bar. For making more friends. In fact, the more candy the better, with a nice selection of nut-free options as a courtesy to your allergy-sensitive friends.
6. Boogers. Lots of them. They put out fires!
7. A knife strapped to your calf and hidden by your boot. For cutting ropes. You never know when you're gonna need to cut ropes. We end up cutting ropes a lot around here.
8. Knowledge of the two-blinks yes, one-blink no language. Duh!
9. A fanny pack for carrying stuff. Crazy, right? Maybe hide it under a bulky shirt so it's not so noticeable you got one.
10. Costumes. For blending in. Moustache optional.

About the Author

Mickey "Mick" Bogerman has lived in Beachwood, North Carolina all his life. Mostly he tries to stay out of trouble, but mostly trouble seems to find him anyway. He has a knack for antagonizing scary creatures and girls, not necessarily in that order.

Mick's favorite subjects in school are science (slime, rockets, bugs, and rocks-- what's not to like?), gym class (running, climbing, throwing-- more stuff to like), and reading (yay Mr. Corcoran lets him read whatever he likes-- like comic books).

Speaking of comic books, Mick's favorites are X-Men, Demon Knights, Spiderman and Batman.

Come Visit Us at
www.SlugPieStories.com

Vote for the next Slug Pie Story

Send in your fan art

Share zombie killing tips and tricks

Print Mick's favorite family recipes

Download study guides for classrooms & book clubs

Learn more about your favorite characters

Sign up for our quarterly newsletter for sneak peeks

And more . . .

We're on social media:

Facebook:

https://www.facebook.com/slugpiestories

Goodreads:

https://www.goodreads.com/author/show/8309407.
Mick_Bogerman

Twitter:

https://twitter.com/slugpiestories

Pinterest:

https://www.pinterest.com/slugpiestoriesl/

Instagram:

https://www.instagram.com/slugpiestoriesllc/

YouTube:

https://www.youtube.com/channel/UCaXlBxq6qkQ
ZqOP2hKEdeFA

While Mick's story is fresh in your mind, would you leave us a review in your favorite review spot?

Goodreads: www.goodreads.com

Amazon: www.amazon.com

Barnes & Noble: www.BN.com

Books A Million: www.booksamillion.com

ACKNOWLEDGEMENTS

This book could not have been created without help and inspiration from the following:

The Blaski Family and The Hockhalter Family for their emotional and financial support.

The extraordinary Jennifer Kay, Alice Fleury, and Dana Nuenighoff for their critiquing, and writerly love.

The Asner Family, The Morris Family, and The Beasley Family for leading the cheer online and in person.

The folks at the Alliance of Independent Authors for their insight and encouragement.

Amy Maddox for editing and proofreading with scalpel precision and tender care.

Kat Powell for her exceptional talent, unending patience, and kick-rumpus illustrations.

To the students who follow their dreams. Their passion is an inspiration.

Nic, Clarissa, and Irina for never-ending curiosity and enthusiasm.

For the writers, too numerous to mention them all, who put themselves out there every day, teaching and motivating the rest of us.

To the readers. You are the reason.

CPSIA information can be obtained
at www.ICGtesting.com
Printed in the USA
FSHW020458230921
84962FS